A Promise to Keep

Sunrise Sisters Trilogy

OLIVIA MILES

ROSEWOOD PRESS

979-8986262451 (print)
A Promise to Keep

also by olivia miles

Sunrise Sisters Trilogy

A Memory So Sweet

A Promise to Keep

A Wish Come True

Blue Harbor Series

A Place for Us

Second Chance Summer

Because of You

Small Town Christmas

Return to Me

Then Comes Love

Finding Christmas

A New Beginning

Summer of Us

A Chance on Me

Evening Island

Meet Me at Sunset

Summer's End

The Lake House

Oyster Bay Series

Feels Like Home

Along Came You

Maybe This Time

This Thing Called Love

Those Summer Nights

Christmas at the Cottage

Still the One

One Fine Day

Had to Be You

Misty Point

One Week to the Wedding

The Winter Wedding Plan

Briar Creek Series

Mistletoe on Main Street

A Match Made on Main Street

Hope Springs on Main Street

Love Blooms on Main Street

Christmas Comes to Main Street

Harlequin Special Edition

'Twas the Week Before Christmas

Recipe for Romance

Sweeter in the City Series

Sweeter in the Summer

Sweeter Than Sunshine

No Sweeter Love

One Sweet Christmas

ONE

Love was in the air—at least for some. Becca Parker knew better than to indulge in feelings of disappointment when she glanced at the clock on the kitchen wall of the Sunrise Sisters Bakery and realized that her one-o'clock cake tasting was about to begin.

Was it a terrible thing to admit that she'd rather be on dish duty than carefully slicing bite-sized portions of cake for the happy couple?

Yes, it was, and that was why she hadn't complained or asked one of her sisters to handle the meeting. Why she'd agreed to the third wedding request this week. And why she had bitten her tongue and smiled when she told her sisters the so-called good news.

Three wedding cake orders in one week were not something to take for granted, not when only a couple of months ago, the "Sunrise Sisters" were on the verge of losing this bakery that had been in their family for generations. Now, thanks to Becca's younger sister Carly's fresh ideas and a strategic mix of old and new recipes, business had never been better.

It was all wonderful, really, just wonderful. Becca's head knew that. But her heart... Well, let's just say that weddings and Becca were two things that didn't mix well. Like oil and water.

With the plate of samples in one hand, she pushed through the swinging door into the storefront with the other. It was a warm, early June day, and the bakery was light and lively. The pastry case gleamed, filled with colorful-looking cupcakes, an assortment of cookies and pastries, three flavors of brownies, a few leftover muffins from the morning, and of course, Nana's famous pies, even if she hadn't personally made them.

Near the cash register where Carly was ringing up coffee and a cinnamon roll, a couple not much younger or older than Becca was standing excitedly, hands clasped, the woman's eyes nearly as shiny as the new brass light fixtures that Becca and her sisters had installed in their recent renovation.

A pang of something close to jealousy, or maybe regret, was quickly nipped in the bud. Becca knew that this wasn't the time to wallow, not in self-pity, and not in wishing for something that couldn't come true. Hard work made sure of that, and this bakery offered plenty of opportunities to keep busy.

Even if it was a daily reminder of the choice she'd made to put her love for this business over her love for—

Right. No thinking about him. Jonah Stone was long

gone. Two years had passed. It was just the bride-to-be stirring up memories that Becca would rather forget.

"You must be the happy couple," she said with a smile. "I'm Becca Parker, one of the co-owners here. I have your tastings, so if you'd like to take a seat, you can try them at your leisure. Once you decide on the flavor, we can go over your ideas for the design."

The bride all but squealed before she and her fiancé dropped into chairs at a table near the window.

Becca set the platter before them and pointed out the flavors. "I can mix and match whatever you like, so don't be shy in asking me to bring out more options. This is your wedding cake and we'll do everything we can to make it perfect."

The engagement finger on the woman's finger sparkled when she reached for the first slice, and Becca realized she was rubbing the bare spot on her own finger, where a similar ring had once sat.

With a tight smile, she left them to it and walked back to the kitchen, wondering if she might be able to ask her sister Jill to handle the next part of the meeting. Jill, however, had just returned from delivering six boxes of assorted pastries to the garden club's monthly lunch and looked weary as she retied her apron strings.

"How was Nana?" Becca asked.

Since retiring from the bakery last year, their grandmother had made herself busy with local clubs and groups. Like her granddaughters, Sharon Parker wasn't one to stay idle.

Becca knew that her grandmother missed waking up

before dawn with the purpose of being at Sunrise in time to roll out pie dough and bake muffins, and she suspected that she would probably end up just like the woman who raised her after her mother passed away. Working here until she couldn't anymore.

"Oh, you know Nana." Jill sighed and pulled a mixing bowl from the shelf. She wasted no time in sliding over the flour and sugar canisters. When it came to the recipes that had been passed down through the generations, they didn't need to look at the recipe, but for their newer additions to the menu, they paid careful attention, knowing that eventually, those recipes would also become an old habit.

And that when they did, it would be a sign to start thinking of new ones. The bakery may have become stale in recent years, but now it was full of fresh hope.

Much like the couple on the other side of the door, picking out their wedding cake.

"Nana's always the life of the party," Becca said, forcing her attention back on the conversation. She pulled a notebook from the drawer near the bulletin board where they wrote down orders and inventory needs, and, lately, new recipe ideas to try in their spare time.

"Seems that she replaces standing out front and greeting all her customers with chatting to anyone who will listen at all the events she attends. I swear, that woman has a better social life than I do and I'm the one in my thirties." Jill measured sugar and poured it into the mixing bowl.

"We're quite the pair," Becca agreed. Since Nana's arthritis forced her into retirement, Jill and Becca had worked tirelessly to keep things going, nearly not succeeding. But now that Carly had come back to join them as a full-time partner at the bakery, the extra set of hands meant that, in theory, they should be less busy.

Instead, Becca felt like they were busier than ever.

"You manage to make it to book club every month," Jill pointed out.

"Ah, but I never do find time to read the book." Becca grinned.

"At this rate, I'll probably never go on another date again." Jill shook her head. "At least you can say—" She stopped herself, looking up from the mixing bowl to meet Becca's eye.

Before she could apologize, Becca held up a hand to stop her. "Don't worry. It's fine."

And it was, almost. At least that's what she told everyone in the days and weeks after Jonah had left town, taking his engagement ring with him. *It's fine*, she'd say, with a forced smile. *He got a wonderful opportunity. I couldn't hold him back.*

And she couldn't go with him either.

Or, to hear him tell it, she wouldn't go with him.

"Speaking of engaged couples, I should probably get back out front soon to see how the tasting is going." *And stop thinking about Jonah.*

She knew that if she asked Jill to take her place that her sister would. That all she had to do was say the word, to share that this stirred up feelings she'd rather not dwell on, hurt that had never quite healed and maybe never would. But that would mean openly admitting that she wasn't fine.

And if she said that to Jill then she would be admitting it to herself.

Really, it was better to just grin and bear it, and work through the pain until one day, she realized that it was gone. She flipped to an open page in her notebook as Carly burst into the kitchen.

"I'm just here for the rest of the flower cookies," Carly said, scanning the counters stacked with cooling racks of baked goods for the sweets she'd made earlier. "And to tell you both some interesting news."

Interesting news and Hope Hollow felt like an oxymoron. In such a small town that Becca had lived in all her life and never left, she was rarely surprised by anything that took place within its borders.

"The space next door is available," Carly announced.

"The bridal shop?" Jill darted a worried glance at Becca.

Becca saw this as the final closure then. She'd never picked up her wedding dress from the boutique and now she never would. Never could. Really, it was for the best.

Still, given that none of them were engaged to be married, she didn't see how this was particularly interesting, much less news, until she saw the way Carly's eyes were lit up and her eyebrows were waggling.

"Oh, no," Jill said, shutting their youngest sister down immediately. "Don't tell me you're thinking that we should take it?"

"It was just a thought..." Carly looked a little deflated.

"We just managed to pull this place out of the red," Jill pointed out.

"And business is booming!" Carly's expression turned excited again. "More space means more customers."

"And more money." Jill raised an eyebrow.

As was often the case, Carly turned to Becca, her big hazel eyes so hopeful that Becca hated the thought of disappointing her.

"It feels nice to catch our breath," Becca said. "And we're barely doing that. The truth is, Carly, I'm not sure how much more we can take on right now. Maybe in a year, we can decide then."

"A year?" Carly started to laugh, but she didn't sound very amused. "That place won't be available in a year. Do you know how long it will take before this opportunity ever comes along again?"

Given that most of the businesses on Main Street were passed down through generations, Becca knew the answer. Well.

"Do we know what they're asking?" Becca asked, pushing her long braid over her shoulder.

"Becca!" Jill sounded more amused than disappointed. She stared frankly at Carly. "It's about more than the upfront cost. We'd have to build the place out. Knock down the adjoining wall. Close this place for work." She blinked a few times as if just the idea of it was too overwhelming.

"Or we hold onto it until we're ready to expand," Carly suggested.

Becca had to admit that wasn't a bad idea. Now, as was also often the case, she turned to Jill. So did Carly.

Their older sister started cracking eggs into a bowl with a little more force than usual.

"We'll think about it, okay?" Jill said.

Carly couldn't fight off her smile as she picked up the tray of cookies and pushed back through the kitchen door. Becca could only shake her head and follow her.

At the table near the window, the plate sitting between the couple was now empty. She swallowed back that emotion again, the one that had been creeping in all week, thanks to all these wedding cake orders. She knew that there would be more, so she'd just have to get used to it.

"Did you come to a decision?" Becca asked. It was often the case, in her experience, that most people didn't dally too long over the cake's flavor. At least she hadn't. But then, she'd been born into a family of bakers, tasting cakes had been her job at an early age when she'd already decided that when she got married, she'd have lemon and raspberry for her filling.

It was the outside of the cake that slowed things down in these meetings. Or in her case, came to a grinding halt. She'd never finished designing her own wedding cake; she'd been too busy with the day-to-day baking. Maybe, that had been a sign.

"They're all so delicious that it's hard to pick just one," the bride said, even though it was clear by the smile in her eyes that a decision had been made. "I think we'll go with the chiffon."

"That's an excellent choice." Becca made a note and then pulled over an extra chair. "You said on the phone that you're expecting one hundred guests?"

Another thing that Becca had never gotten around to when planning her wedding: the guest list. When the engagement was called off, she realized that was just as well. No invitations had been sent, minimizing the awkwardness.

Of course, it didn't stop the spread of pity that seemed to blow down Main Street like a cold winter breeze. For months after the split, she couldn't hand over a mug of coffee or a slice of pie without seeing what she'd come to refer to as "the look" in everyone's eyes.

Jilted. That was the word that she heard being whispered when people thought she couldn't hear. Left behind. Betrayed. Heartbroken.

Only some of it was true, though, but Becca didn't see a reason to correct anyone, even when she was sometimes tempted. Everyone, including her family, thought that Jonah had broken her heart.

But the truth of the matter was that she'd broken his, too.

"Have you given any more thought to the space next door?" Carly asked, once the after-school rush was over and the end of the day was drawing near.

It was another successful afternoon, judging from the near-empty display case. It was customary for the bakery to donate the leftovers to a community center or local cause, but these days, they rarely had anything to offer.

It was a good problem to have, Becca thought. It meant that they were selling nearly everything they made, and some days, all of it. It would be a poor business decision to over-produce, but she still felt bad when she realized that it had been a couple of weeks since she'd made any drop-offs on her way home after a long, hard day.

Becca stopped wiping a table and looked at her younger sister across the room. Since returning to town, Carly was full of new ideas for the bakery, which sometimes led to tension.

"You know we can't do anything without Jill's approval," Becca reminded her.

"She's not our boss," Carly replied. "All three of us run the place. That's why we renamed it Sunrise Sisters Bakery, not Jill's Bakery."

Becca laughed but stopped when Jill pushed through the kitchen door.

"What's so funny?" she asked.

Becca knew better than to share the joke. Jill had always been the more serious of the sisters, and contrary to what *some* thought, she cared the most about this bakery.

Even though Becca had also put it above all else.

"Do you need me to stay and prep tonight?" Carly asked, clearly hoping that the answer would be no. Becca was fully aware that Carly intended to spend the evening with her boyfriend, Nick Sutton, and his sweet little daughter Daisy.

"Seeing as you're the only one of us with a personal life, go," Jill told her. "I have nothing to get home to, so I may as well stay."

"Hey, you have me," Becca teased. They'd been sharing a small cottage near the center of town for a couple of years now, though most of their waking hours were spent here at the bakery.

"I'd offer to stay and help, but I have a delivery to drop

off for the town hall meeting tonight," Becca said. She glanced at the lingering customers and checked the time on the watch she still wore, even though Jonah had bought it for her for Christmas one year. It was a functional decision to wear it, not a sentimental one, but still, she couldn't fight the pull of her heart when she remembered the grin in his eyes as she'd opened it.

"It's fine. It gives me something to do. It's that or a pile of laundry waiting for me at home." Jill gave a good-natured shrug before going back into the kitchen.

"Jill's already putting in long hours at the bakery," Becca told Carly. "I don't think we can really convince her to take on more responsibility just now."

A smile curved Carly's mouth as she came to stand closer, lowering her voice so they wouldn't be overheard. "So you're not opposed to the idea?"

Becca hesitated. "The timing isn't ideal, but then, opportunities like this don't come along very often."

She swallowed hard, realizing what she'd said. The echo of Jonah's announcement when he'd been given a chef position at a top LA restaurant.

The way for years he would lament the lack of space on Main Street that made it impossible for his parents to ever open the restaurant they'd dreamed of—or for Jonah to live out that wish for them.

Shaking away the memories, she said, "I have to stop by the town hall and that's right near the real estate office. Why don't I pop in and feel things out? Then we'll know if this conversation is even worth continuing."

Carly all but jumped up and down and Becca could only

shake her head and laugh. She walked behind the counter to fetch the box of pastries she'd set aside earlier and then pushed out the front door onto the sidewalk, taking a peek at the darkened storefront next door that didn't yet have a sign in the window.

June was one of her favorite months in Hope Hollow. The days were longer and warmer, and the flowers were in full bloom. Their Connecticut town was equally charming in autumn when the maple trees boasted their blazing colors, and during the holiday season when the entire town seemed to sparkle under a blanket of snow.

But there was something special about summer days, full sun and blue skies, that always made her feel like anything was possible.

Maybe even expanding the business.

The town hall wasn't far, nestled directly in the center of Main Street across from the square with its historical gazebo and a statue of the founding father. Becca handed over the box of pastries to the mayor's assistant and realized once again that she never tired to see the lift of someone's spirits when they popped open a bakery box and saw the goodies inside.

Then, because she was a little curious, and at least wanted to know all the facts before she wasted her time imagining something more for her life, she stopped inside the real estate office next door.

Erika McCoy was coming down the hall, and she gave a friendly wave. A fellow book club member, Erika was also a real estate agent, and she'd been one of Becca's neighbors when the sisters had all moved in with Nana as children.

"This is a surprise. Don't tell me that you're planning to sell the bakery!"

Not so long ago, that had been exactly what Becca and Jill had planned, or at least, considered. Now, Becca felt confident and relieved to shake her head. "No, nothing like that. Actually, I was here about the space next door. The bridal shop?"

Erika set down the open house sign she'd been holding and sighed.

"Sometimes I think wrestling these things is more difficult than wrangling my little boys," she said with a laugh.

Erika and her two children stopped in every few weeks for cookies and hot chocolate, especially in the winter months. Still, it surprised Becca that someone her age could be so settled in life, that Erika was managing to balance a career and a family life, while Becca had been forced to pick just one.

"Is the space still available?" Becca asked.

"For now, but I doubt it will sit for long." Erika tilted her head. "Why? Are you interested in expanding?"

"That depends on the price," Becca said with a chuckle.

"Well, I should tell you that we've already had some interest in the place," Erika warned her.

For reasons she couldn't explain, Becca felt her heart sink with disappointment. It was silly, she knew, to think that they could even entertain the idea of actually pouring more money into this business, but the thought of the possibility being taken away made everything feel more permanent. That the bakery would only ever be what it currently was. That her entire life was already cemented.

And limited.

She pushed back the thought of the choices she'd made, the options she'd let pass, the opportunity she'd turned down, and focused on this one.

"But if you're interested, you'd have to go over the list price."

There was no way Jill would go for that.

Still, Becca couldn't fight the nerves that pulled at her stomach. She'd put everything she had into the bakery, committing to it, putting her loyalty to the past over her dreams of the future.

Was now the time to double-down? Confirm that she'd made the right decision all those years ago by not going to California with Jonah?

Or would that just lead to more risk, and maybe even more heartache?

Or worse. Maybe, if she put even more time, energy, and money into the bakery, she wouldn't be proving that she'd made the right choice.

Maybe, she'd be ensuring that she'd never have time for anything else. Or anyone else.

"I'm actually surprised that you didn't already know," Erika said, frowning a little.

"Oh, I usually slip in and out through the back kitchen door," Becca started to say, not just because it made sense, but because passing the boutique was a reminder she didn't need.

"I meant about the offer..." Erika darted her eyes to something over Becca's shoulder. "There's the interested party now," she said, looking both nervous and a little excited as she licked her lip.

Becca wished she'd never come in. She wasn't in a position to make an offer on the spot.

But as the person behind her approached and she turned to see who it was, she realized that the light in Erika's eyes had nothing at all to do with the empty storefront and everything to do with the two people who wanted it.

two

"Jonah."

Becca felt the air stall in her lungs as her heart began to pound. It was the only sound left in the lobby, which had gone eerily still. Even Erika had stopped clicking her pen, and from the looks of it, Jonah hadn't blinked in about as many seconds as she had.

"Bec." He said the word on a breath, barely audible, but it was there. The nickname he alone used for her.

She pushed away the small part of her heart that was still reserved just for him and for all the memories they had made together. The part of her that she'd closed off, along with the dreams that they'd once shared, replaced in time with other plans.

Like the one that had brought her here today.

Jonah Stone was the other interested party, once again standing in the way of her hopes for herself and her loyalty to her family.

"Well, this is awkward," Erika said in a singsong voice to cover her discomfort.

Jonah cracked a smile, but Becca realized with horror that she was blinking back tears. This wasn't just awkward. This was downright confusing.

When Jonah had left for LA, he'd made it clear that it was for good reason. An opportunity of a lifetime. One that didn't come along often and maybe never would again. A chance to break out in the industry, to pad his resume, to learn under the best.

Gone was the dream of opening a restaurant here in Hope Hollow. Gone was the plan of buying a starter home and building a life together.

Gone was the wedding. And the ring. And everything he'd said that he wanted, for years.

But gone was not the bakery. Jonah might have been willing to walk away from everything he'd once claimed to cherish, including her, but she wasn't.

She lifted her chin a notch, the tears drying up as quickly as that little soft spot in her chest.

"You're...back in town?" An obvious question with a not-so-obvious answer.

She'd expected him to come back for the occasional visit, if not to see her then his grandfather. Mr. Quincy was a sweet old man, and all alone since his wife died and not long after, his only daughter, Jonah's mother.

But Jonah wasn't here for a visit. No, he was back as in back to stay. At least for now.

Because if there was one thing that she'd learned about Jonah, it was that he didn't keep his promises for long.

He nodded, having the nerve to even grin a little wider. "Here I am."

Her lip curled. If he was expecting her to throw her arms around his neck or call out the welcome wagon in his honor, he could dream on.

"Funny," she remarked, tipping her head. "I seem to remember you having... What did you call it?" She gave a dramatic pause. "Oh, that's right. An *opportunity of a lifetime* in Los Angeles."

Erika gave a strange little sound that was a cross between a laugh and squeak and said, "You know, I just remembered that I have a call to make." She was already stepping away, her shoulders shaking in a nervous way, before she suddenly turned on her patent leather heel and all but sprinted down the hallway.

Very soon, a door could be heard closing, loudly. A second later, though, Becca could have sworn she heard it open again.

She briefly shut her eyes. The talk in town would be relentless. She'd only finally stopped getting the pity glances, and now she was sure to be met with wide eyes from the nosy but well-intentioned locals who were eager to know how she was going to handle Jonah being back in their small New England town.

"Well, that was awkward," Jonah said, keeping up the grin, though it had slipped a little.

She kept her own expression stone-faced. "It doesn't have to be awkward. But you taking the space next to the bakery certainly would be."

Seriously, what had he been thinking? Coming back here was one thing, but working next door, day after day?

"You know how long I waited for a space to open up on that street," he said, all joking aside now.

She did know. Not just because it had been his hope, but his parents' too. Sometimes, in the days after he'd moved, she wondered what might have happened if it had been easier for him to fulfill that dream here.

But then she reminded herself that he'd given up on it. And her.

"I was planning to stop by to tell you," Jonah was saying. "I was just waiting for the right time."

"And when was that going to be? The day you opened for business? Or after I found out through the local grapevine?"

"I only got in yesterday," he explained.

"You could have called," she said.

He raised an eyebrow. "Would you have picked up?"

Probably not, she thought, but once, in the days and weeks after their breakup, she might have. Her doubts were so strong, it wouldn't have taken much to make her reconsider her decision to stay here in Hope Hollow. But he'd never called. Or pushed. He'd accepted her answer to be final, and she'd done the same.

Assumed he'd never come back. Yet here he was.

"And what about your fabulous life in LA?" she asked now.

She didn't know anything about his life on the West Coast, clearly. She'd just assumed that it was everything he'd hoped it would be and more. It had kept him away, without so much as a visit, for two years. And it had taken him away from her, too.

Now, she considered that he might have a girlfriend. He might even be engaged. Maybe that's what he was doing. Coming home to fulfill the plan he'd once made...with someone else.

"I have my reasons for coming back," he said. "And the vacant space on Main Street is only one of them."

Becca pursed her lips. His grandfather was getting up there in age, and he'd recently lost his old black Lab. It all but broke the poor man's heart, and even the newfound company of Becca's grandmother, or her endless offering of sweets, couldn't heal that wound.

There were some things in life that nothing could fix, but Jonah being back would certainly cheer up Mr. Quincy.

Jonah stuffed his hands into his pockets and gave her a long look, one that made her heart lift and then drop, one that made her remember the softness of his grey eyes, the strong line of his jaw, the fullness of those lips she'd once kissed, and the connection that they'd once shared.

"It doesn't have to be awkward between us, Bec. I don't want it to."

She nodded. No, she didn't want that either. It felt sad to be standing here, barely knowing what to say or where to begin with a man with whom she'd once shared so much and intended to share even more. If he hadn't decided to move to LA, and if she hadn't decided to stay in Hope Hollow, then right now it might have been the two of them standing in this real estate office, excitedly putting in an offer on their first house, instead of inquiring about the same property that they intended to use separately.

They would have already been married. Maybe, they would have even had a baby by now, or one on the way.

Instead, she felt like she no longer even knew him. Or what he'd experienced for the past two years, in a place she'd never visited.

"What do you want then?" she asked, because he'd never been shy in expressing that, not when he'd proposed, and not when he'd snatched all their plans out from under her by announcing his intentions to leave.

He shrugged, even though it was clear his mind was made up—for now.

"I want to move back to town. Open a neighborhood restaurant. Live happily ever after."

Her eyes hooded. In other words, everything he'd once wanted. Only this time, without her.

"Well," she said as her heart began to pound again. "You might have to find another spot for your new bistro or gastropub or whatever it is you're planning these days. You're not the only interested party in the vacancy on Main Street."

His brow furrowed. "But you already have a business."

"And why shouldn't we think about expanding it?" she countered.

His eyes flashed as a little grunt of surprise escaped from his mouth. "You'd really do that to me?"

She hesitated, but only for a second. She knew how badly he wanted that dream. But she also saw how easily he'd given it up.

"It's not always about you and your plans, Jonah. That storefront is next to the bakery, which is thriving, by the way," she added, giving a little smile.

Jonah stared at her, stunned, and Erika, who had clearly been listening to every word of this conversation from a safe distance, used the opportunity to hustle back to the lobby, her eyes eager.

"Hello again, you two," she said, flicking a nervous glance at each of them. "Now, Becca, you had asked about the old wedding dress shop and I wanted to hand you the listing sheet."

"But I already made an offer on the property," Jonah said firmly and quickly.

Becca took the sheet and nailed him with a hard look before skimming the information. Size. Terms. Description. Price.

She managed not to gulp and only because there were two sets of eyes on her.

"And what happens if the bakery decides to make an offer too?" she asked, feeling the blood begin to rush in her ears. There was no way Jill would go for this. But there was no way that Becca could let Jonah waltz back into town and take a part of her dream again, even if it was one that she hadn't exactly realized she wanted until this morning.

Erika's eyes lit up. "In that case, there would be a bidding war."

And this time, Becca did gulp.

"I'll need to discuss this with my sisters," she said, forcing herself not to even glance in Jonah's direction.

"Of course!" Erika nodded excitedly. "I'll let the owner know to expect a second offer."

"This hardly seems fair," Jonah said, frowning deeply.

"Nothing's fair when it comes to business," Erika said with a light laugh.

Or love, Becca thought, as she gave one last glance at Jonah and pushed out the door.

Jonah sat in his car on Main Street, watching Becca until she disappeared from view.

He'd known this moment was coming, braced himself for it even. Making the decision to come back to Hope Hollow was the easy part, preparing to see his fiancée was another.

Make that ex-fiancée.

Two years. It was hard to believe that was how long it had been since they'd last seen each other, or even spoken.

Almost as hard as it was to believe that now they had spoken again, and it hadn't gone anything like he'd planned.

For several reasons.

He turned the key in the ignition, eager to get away from the real estate office before he went back in and did something stupid, like pull his offer on the empty storefront. The storefront he'd waited for years to become available. The space that had felt like destiny just forty-eight hours ago, if he believed in fate and all that. Which he didn't. Life was full of too many surprises—some of them nasty—to ever lead him to believe that things happened for a reason, or were predestined. If there was such a thing as fate, then one of two things should have happened by now: he and Becca should have been married, or his big career opportunity in Los Angeles should have been just that.

Or long ago, a space like this would have come along.

Long enough for his parents to have seen it.

But none of that had happened. He'd been used to the hard road, but he'd never given up the dream, just buried it instead. Told himself to stop waiting for it. To get on with life.

The job in California seemed like the answer. Instead, he'd put in long days, cooking other people's recipes, learning a few things, sure, but all at the cost of his creativity.

And the only woman he'd ever loved.

The drive to his grandfather's house was short, and when he pulled to a stop in the driveway, he glanced over at the Colonial next door, thinking of all the times he used to see Becca outside, back when they were kids, and he'd make up an excuse to stop over, even if it meant tossing his ball over the fence. By the time they were in their late teens, he didn't need an excuse. Just the courage to ask her one hot summer day if she wanted to get ice cream, even though they'd had ice cream together dozens of times by then. But maybe she'd felt the shift too—from neighbors to friends to something more. It had all been so easy with Bec. So comforting.

So wonderful.

Tearing his gaze from her grandmother's house, Jonah let himself in the side door, surprised as much today as he was yesterday morning when he'd first arrived to be greeted by silence instead of the barking of a dog, welcoming him.

He frowned when he saw the old dog bed near the radiator, knowing that his grandfather wasn't ready to part with it just yet. He'd been through loss before, Jonah knew. But that didn't mean it got easier.

He found his grandfather in the living room, sitting in his easy chair, watching a game show.

Hoping to cheer the man up, Jonah said, "I was wondering if you were next door with your girlfriend!"

Now his grandfather slid him a rueful look but it was clear the man was pleased. He'd only been chasing Sharon Parker for the last decade—or more—and had finally worn her down with his advances.

Not to mention his big heart.

Jonah settled onto the couch. He was very aware that his grandfather was watching him, waiting.

Was it that obvious? Jonah sighed.

"I saw Becca."

His grandfather's mouth twitched but he didn't react further. "It was bound to happen."

Jonah nodded. "Yep. It was."

Just not like that.

"So," his grandfather said in his deep voice. Behind his spectacles, his eyes glimmered. "Did you tell her about the new restaurant?"

"Not in so many words," Jonah said grimly. Now he wondered if there would even be a new restaurant. If once again, their plans would clash, canceling each other out.

Canceling *them* out.

"But she knows you're back and not just visiting?" There was a hint of uncertainty in his grandfather's voice, confirmation that this time, Jonah wasn't going anywhere.

"Oh, she knows all right," Jonah said with a sigh. The announcement just hadn't gone as planned. But then, he couldn't name one thing in his life that had.

"And does she know why?" his grandfather pressed.

Jonah shook his head. Telling Becca that he'd regretted ever leaving Hope Hollow was a conversation for another day. A day when she was willing to listen—if it would even happen now.

He could see the impatience on his grandfather's face when he said, "Take it from me, kid. Don't take too long to make things right with her. Time has a way of sneaking up on us."

Jonah knew that his grandfather was right. And he'd always been the type to seize the day, to make the most of things, to spend the present building for the future.

Now, with the issue of the empty storefront on Main Street, that no longer felt like such an easy task. And as for getting into the reasons for returning to town, he was no longer so sure that Becca was willing to sit and hear him out, or if she even cared.

But she understood him. She knew him. Better than anyone—better than the old man sitting in this room, looking at him with kind eyes.

Becca knew what that storefront meant to him. Had she forgotten that? Or didn't she care?

He swallowed back that worry and focused on what he could control. Cooking wasn't just his career, it was also his passion. His greatest love, or so Becca liked to say, once fondly. Now, probably not so much.

When he was in the kitchen, doing his thing, all the other problems in his life seemed to fade away, and he was right back beside his parents, the radio playing, the pans sizzling, and the counter overflowing with ingredients.

Even if it was only in spirit.

"It's getting late. Why don't I make us some dinner?" he offered.

"As long as it's nothing too fancy," his grandfather warned. "Save that stuff for your new restaurant."

His new restaurant. Yesterday it had felt so certain. Now, he wasn't even sure it was something he still wanted. Not when once again, it meant taking something from the only girl he'd ever loved.

"I'll make one of your favorites," he promised. Meaning, he'd make something his mother used to make, an old recipe she'd learned from his grandmother. Before he moved to California, he used to cook for his grandfather all the time, old staples that he'd grown up on, usually reserved for nights when his parents' restaurant was closed.

"Sharon Parker must be a pretty good cook," he hedged, even though he knew that Becca's grandmother was more of a baker. Still, she knew her way around a kitchen, which was more than he could say for his grandfather.

"No one bakes cinnamon rolls like Sharon." Sure enough, his grandfather smiled. "But no one could cook like your mother. Not even your grandmother, rest her soul."

"Not even me?" Jonah was amused. But there was sadness there too. When he was away, it was easier somehow not to think about the family he'd lost.

Not to miss them.

"Your mother would be darn proud of you," his grandfather said in response to that.

Jonah wasn't so sure of that and the unease returned, reminding him of how he'd tried and failed to carry on his parents' legacy. But he had another chance now. And he wasn't sure when the opportunity would come around again.

And the one person standing in the way of his dream was Becca of all people. When once, she'd shared it.

Knowing that there was nothing more that he could do about that at the moment, he stood and stretched his back. His shoulders still felt tense from the unexpected turn to his day.

"I've been working out a twist on some classics—"

But his grandfather just gave him a wary look. "Why mess with a good thing, Jonah?"

There was probably another meaning under the surface, an implication that Jonah had gone and done just that, even though his grandfather had never tried to stop him or make him feel guilty for moving across the country. He'd had a good thing here. A great thing really.

But it hadn't felt like enough. Now, he wondered if it ever would be, if he didn't get a storefront on Main Street.

"How am I going to perfect my recipes if I don't have you to taste test for me?" he joked.

His grandfather only shook his head. "I'm a simple guy, Jonah. I don't need all those fancy ingredients you loaded into my fridge and pantry. I'm just happy with a hot meal, a warm house, and the love of a good woman." He winked but there was sadness in his smile and Jonah knew that there was one thing he hadn't named in that list. The companionship of a loyal friend.

Jonah managed to laugh as he walked back into the kitchen and began pulling the so-called fancy ingredients from the cabinet. He looked out the window over the sink, to where Becca's grandmother lived, wondering if she was home, if she'd heard yet that he was back. But no, if she had, she would have told Becca, and the shock on Becca's face when she saw him today proved that she was just as surprised to be face-to-face as he was.

He'd known it was coming. But not like this.

Now he could only hope for a second chance.

For the dream he'd once had.

three

By the next morning, Becca wasn't sure how much longer she could hold in the news that not only was Jonah back in town but that he was bidding on the space next door.

And oh, that's right. So were they.

She eyed Jill across the workbench, feeling guilty that her older sister was none the wiser, engrossed in her morning task of mixing scone batter, going about her day without a clue as to what Becca had been up to yesterday afternoon while Jill was prepping for today.

She glanced at the clock. Of all days, Carly was running late.

"Is Carly coming in today?" she asked Jill, hoping her tone was conversational and not as desperate as it felt. She'd given in to Carly's idea, and now she wished she hadn't. That she'd never walked into that real estate office. Never seen Jonah. Never felt her heart break open all over again.

But then if she hadn't seen him yesterday, she'd likely

have seen him today. Or tomorrow. There would be no avoiding him in a town this small.

Certainly not if he was working next door to the bakery.

Jill didn't stop working; very little caused Jill to ever stop mid-task. She never slipped up on a measurement, never added too much salt or sugar, or got the two mixed up, either. She prided herself on reliable recipes and a strong effort.

"She didn't say she wasn't. Besides," Jill said, briefly glancing at the clock. "We got in early. She's not exactly late."

That was a good point, and one that Becca had overlooked in her mostly sleepless night. By the time the clock hit four, she was relieved to have an excuse to be out of bed, to have somewhere to go, a distraction from her mind that wouldn't stop replaying her exchange with Jonah, and everything that had led up to it, too.

Becca began scooping her muffin mixture into the tin. By the time she had the first batch in the oven, the back door opened and Carly walked in, bringing a gust of cool, fresh air with her that was always appreciated in the kitchen, which grew warmer with each passing hour of the day.

Carly wasted no time setting her expensive handbag better matched for her city-living days on a hook and tying on an apron.

"You two are here early!" she remarked. Then, her eyes went to Becca. "Did I miss anything?"

Oh, a lot, Becca thought. So much so that she wasn't sure where to start.

But now Jill was going over the specials of the day,

repeating them for Carly, even though they were posted on the board, and Becca was starting to lose her nerve. Jill wasn't her boss, just her older sister, but she'd taken on the brunt of the work in the bakery all her life, even though Becca sometimes felt like she'd been the one to sacrifice the most.

"How was your evening with Nick and Daisy?" Becca started on the second batch of muffins. They could hardly keep the blueberry ones from selling out by nine most days.

As usual when asked about Nick, Carly's cheeks flushed. There was no doubt that she was happy for the second chance with her first love, and even happier by the addition of a daughter from his brief marriage.

"Daisy is starting summer camp next week. Dance camp. She has a new tutu and put on a little performance for us," Carly smiled fondly as she grabbed some pie dough from the fridge and brought it back to the counter.

"I'm happy for you," Becca said, meaning it, even as a little piece of her heart started to ache. Some people were meant to find their way back together after circumstances drove them apart. Others not so much.

"So..." Carly gave her a less-than-subtle look before glancing at Jill. She floured the marble worktop before unwrapping the dough and then began rolling it into a flat circle for the morning quiches.

Becca swallowed hard, knowing that there was no avoiding what had happened yesterday after closing up shop.

"I stopped by the real estate office after the town hall yesterday," she said, going for casual, but the tightening of her throat gave away her nerves as she waited for Jill's response. Sure enough, her sister gave a little sigh and a shake of her head.

"And what did you discover? That the price is sky high?" Jill asked.

"There's already an offer on the property," she said, watching Carly's face fold in dismay.

"See!" Carly shot an accusatory glance at Jill. "I told you it would go fast and we couldn't on this opportunity. Did Erika say who was interested?"

"She didn't have to say, because he walked in while I was talking to her." Just thinking about the shock she felt at seeing Jonah made Becca shudder a little.

"Well?" Carly sounded impatient. "Who was it?"

Becca set down the mixing spoon and looked at both of her sisters. "Jonah."

Now she had both of their attention, including Jill's.

"Jonah?" Carly gasped. "But...but..." She turned to Jill to finish her thought, but Jill stood stone-faced, digesting the news, and clearly none too happy about it.

"I know," was all Becca could reply. Because she knew everything her sisters were probably thinking right now. She'd thought of it all last night. And this morning.

"Did you guys...talk?" Jill asked hesitantly.

"You could call it that." Becca shook her head. "He intends to open a new restaurant in the space next door."

"Without consulting you?" Carly looked outraged on Becca's behalf, and for a moment, Becca almost smiled.

"Since when has Jonah consulted me on plans when it comes to his career?" *Or his priorities*, she thought to herself.

"So what did you say?" Jill asked.

This was where things got tricky. Becca took a big breath and let it out, almost afraid to even look at her older sister.

"I...said that we were interested in the space too."

"You didn't!" both sisters cried at the same time, one in upset, the other in pure delight.

Becca looked witheringly at Jill. "What could I say? Carly's right, that space won't sit for long. It won't even sit through the end of the day if Jonah has his way. I hated the thought of him thinking he could just waltz into town and pick up where he left off nearly as much as I hated the thought that he might once again stand in the way of my plan for the future. Because this bakery is my future, or at least a part of it."

Lately, it was all of it. Gone were the days of wedding planning and imagining their honeymoon. And later came the other losses—the house, the kids, the thought of coming home to each other each night. She'd poured her heart even deeper into this bakery, this kitchen, to the recipes that had been in her family for generations.

To the one thing she could still hold on to.

Jill pulled in a sigh. "I hear you and I agree with you, but we don't even know what they're asking."

Becca walked over to her own, more modest handbag, and pulled out the listing sheet. She handed it to Jill while Carly looked on over her shoulder.

"This is a lot," Jill said with a cluck of her tongue.

"Unfortunately, with two interested parties, it also goes to a bidding war." Becca cringed.

"Well, what choice do we have? It's ours for the taking! We're not really going to hand it over to Jonah, are we?"

Carly demanded. She narrowed her eyes at the mere thought.

Becca was once again reminded of why she'd made her choice, impossible as it felt at the time. Jonah had been willing to walk away from her, but her sisters always had her back.

Jill studied the listing sheet and then let out another, deeper sigh. "Let's get through the morning rush and then talk later. If we don't get that pastry case filled, we won't have a business left to consider expanding!"

Carly slid Becca a little smile as she went back to rolling out her pie crust.

But Becca had yet to see how any good could come out of this scenario.

"He's here," Carly announced twenty minutes after they'd opened, the kitchen door swinging closed behind her.

She didn't need to say whom she was referring to—it was obvious. Jill was working the front counter today, along with Carly's help, and Becca had assumed that she was safe in the kitchen.

But right now, she didn't even feel safe in her hometown.

She calmly set down the bowl she was holding for fear of dropping it if she didn't. She supposed a part of her knew that Jonah would stop by; they hadn't exactly left things on clear terms yesterday. He'd be making a push for the space next door. Focusing on his plans, and his career. His visit would have nothing to do with her personally.

Or so she tried telling herself.

"I can tell him you're not here," Carly offered. "Or I can tell him where to go."

Despite the emotions roiling through her stomach, Becca laughed. It was tempting to have her little sister stick up for her, but that would just delay the inevitable. And the last thing Becca wanted was to bump into Jonah at the bookstore, where they'd loved spending a few quiet hours looking over the new cookbooks, or at Nana's house, considering that his grandfather lived just next door.

"It's fine," she said. Fine, just fine. Fine when she'd handed over the ring. Fine when she'd called off her wedding. Fine when she'd watched the only man she'd ever loved choose a career over a life with her, even if he'd accused her of the very same.

Fine to now be walking toward the kitchen door, knowing that he was on the other side of it.

She took a steadying breath and, with one push, lifted her chin, squared her shoulders, and stepped into the shopfront, where her heart instantly betrayed her.

He was standing in front of the display case, his hands thrust in the pockets of his jeans, the chest she'd once rested her cheek against when they'd curl up on the couch together to watch their favorite cooking programs now pressing against the soft cotton of his T-shirt. His brown hair, which had always been worn a little long, fell over his forehead, and when he straightened up, turned and faced her, his grey eyes seemed to be clearer than ever.

She realized that she'd stopped walking. That the

distance between them was now only a few feet but it still felt like thousands of miles.

"This is a surprise," she said lightly. And while that wasn't entirely true, she still couldn't quite get over the shock of seeing him in her place of business after all these years.

It was one thing to run into Jonah in town. Another for him to seek her out.

"I didn't like the way we left things yesterday."

And I didn't like the way we left things two years ago, Becca thought.

She nodded, unsure of what to say, because really, what was there to say? Jonah had come back to town, without telling her, and now they were going to have to play nice.

Or maybe not...

She folded her arms. "Which part of how we left things yesterday didn't you like?"

"All of it," Jonah said with a shrug. His eyes turned a little pleading. "I didn't want our first interaction to be like that."

She felt herself soften, but only a little. It would be all too easy to let her guard down around Jonah, to forget the heartache she'd felt when he'd pulled their shared dream out from under her.

"The bakery looks great." Jonah looked around the room, clearly liking what he saw. "When did you renovate?"

"Recently," she said, not wanting to give much away. But then, considering that her grandmother and his grandfather were dating, she added, "Nana retired, if you haven't heard."

He nodded. She wondered what else he knew about her family—or her. Like did he know that she was still single, and hadn't even had so much as a date since the day their engagement ended? It wasn't for lack of effort on the part of the matchmakers in town, the customers who popped in for a coffee and were sure to mention their son the doctor, or their nephew, the attorney.

"Seems like you and your sisters have sunk a lot of money into this place," he commented.

She tipped her head. "We had a lot of help with the renovations from friends in town willing to roll up their shirtsleeves. That's the great thing about Hope Hollow. People here really stand by each other."

He picked up on the slight, his mouth thinning. For a moment, Becca felt bad for turning the conversation unpleasant again, but something told her he hadn't stopped by at this hour just to buy a muffin and go down memory lane.

"Are you really serious about expanding into the space next door?"

And there it was.

"Why wouldn't we be?" She hoped that her expression was more neutral than the anger pumping her blood.

"You have a great setup here. Why change a good thing?"

Oh, he didn't just say that.

"That's a good question," she said, lifting an eyebrow. "Why would anyone want to change a good thing?"

He huffed out a breath. Clearly, he wasn't up for a conversation about their relationship any more than she was. "You know I always wanted a restaurant in town. It took years for a space to open up and it could take years for that to happen again."

"I'm sorry, but last I checked, you wanted to work at some famous restaurant in Los Angeles. Now you suddenly remember the dream you had first and you expect me, of all people, to put aside my plans and opportunities?" She would have laughed if she didn't feel like crying.

"Plans can change," he said.

"Oh, don't I know!" she shot back.

"I mean, that I was open to something new. You were the one chained to the past instead of looking toward the future," he insisted, his eyes hardening.

Gritting her teeth, Becca glanced over at the front of the counter, where Carly was plating a scone for a customer. She paused long enough to give Jonah a death stare.

"I have to get to work, Jonah," Becca said. They were falling back on old arguments, and like before, it wouldn't change a damn thing, only open up wounds she'd thought had finally healed. "We've just opened for the day and we'll have a line backed up to where we're standing before long."

"So that's how we're going to leave things?" He didn't show any sign of moving.

Becca let out an exasperated sigh. She was eager to get away from him, back to the kitchen, but not for the reason she'd stated. Standing here, looking at him, made her feel things she shouldn't, like the smell of his shirt, the heat of his neck, the taste of his mouth.

She glanced over at Jill, who was loading another tray of assorted pastries into the glass case. They locked eyes for a minute, and in them, Becca saw not just support but something deeper. Something the man standing in front of her couldn't offer her. Love.

"My sisters need me, Jonah."

It was the same thing she'd said to him all those years ago: my family needs me. She couldn't leave Nana and Jill to run the bakery, not when Nana's arthritis was getting worse. Not when Carly had long since left town with no intention of returning.

Not when these four walls, where she'd lived nearly as many hours as her childhood home, were all that remained of her mother and the memories they'd made here.

He nodded. "I'll go."

She watched, waiting, to see if he'd say anything more. Instead, he gave a little smile, waved at Jill and Carly, who didn't return the gesture, and walked back out the front door, pausing only to let three women carrying yoga mats enter.

Now, like before, it was so easy for him to walk away.

Becca went back into the kitchen—her safe place, where only family ever entered, and only good things were made. Jill was the one to slide through the door with her.

"I think we should go for the space," she said, forcing Becca to spin around and look at her.

Becca startled. This was the last thing she expected to hear. Well, other than Jonah being back in town.

Jill was cautious, risk-averse, and far less optimistic than their other sister.

"What? But...but the money." Becca's mind was still reeling from the conversation with Jonah, and her heart was still pounding against her ribs. Now she tried to focus on her sister, on what she was proposing. "Let's take the emotion out of it."

But Jill's blue eyes were gleaming. "We're turning a big profit now, and we can always pay ourselves a little less. So things will be tight again for a while. It isn't like we haven't experienced that before."

Becca was tempted, but just remembering the stress she and Jill felt all last winter made her shake her head.

"No, Jill. It's not practical." She rarely had to take this role with her sister, but today, it was necessary. Jill was being protective, feeling all the emotions that Becca was now determined to contain.

Hopefully, to forget.

"I think we should seriously consider it," Jill said firmly.

"But we just got things back on track." Becca gave her sister a hard look, knowing that Jill hadn't forgotten the months of struggle they'd shared after Nana retired. Customers who had been coming for Nana's company rather than her baked goods stopped frequenting the business, and then one of the ovens decided to stop working, leaving them short-handed, overworked, and underpaid. It was only since Carly moved back and they'd decided to modernize both the menu and the interior of the shop that things had turned around.

"We only just bought that new oven," she stressed. And they were still overworked. And even slightly underpaid, considering they put everything back into the business. "Taking on extra space would just mean committing even more to the bakery."

"And what else are we committing to?" Jill countered.

Becca grew silent. Once, she'd committed to Jonah.

"If you're saying this to show I have your support, it's okay. I'm over Jonah. It was for the best that we broke up."

Jill pursed her lips and refilled a tray with chocolate-chip scones that had been cooling on a rack. Soon, the tables would be filled with people enjoying a steaming cup of coffee with the daily paper, and a line would form down the display case, where muffins, pastries, and coffee cake would be carefully selected.

Carly poked her head around the door and glanced back at the counter to make sure no new customers had arrived. Glancing from Jill to Becca, she said, "Did I miss anything?"

Becca began cracking eggs into a bowl for another quiche, knowing that today's flavor—spinach and feta—was popular and always sold out fast. Her hands were still shaking from her interaction with Jonah.

The nerve of that man! To show up here after all this time, to think he could once again make plans without any consideration to what she might want!

"I was telling Becca that I think we should seriously consider the space next door," Jill said, sparking a look of surprise from Carly.

Becca cleared her throat. "Before you go and get too excited, I told her that if this is because Jonah already made an offer, thank you but no thank you. We shouldn't be basing our life around what Jonah chooses to do with his."

She cracked an egg into the bowl a little harder than usual, causing some shells to fall into the mixture, dammit.

Carly and Jill fell silent, along with Becca. But Becca knew that they weren't just thinking about expanding the bakery. They were thinking about how once, Jonah had expected Becca to do just that: to base her life around his, to give up her dreams and hopes. To walk away from this bakery. And her family.

Well, she hadn't done it then and she certainly wouldn't do it now. Whatever they did would be in the best interest of this business and each other.

It would have absolutely nothing to do with Jonah.

four

After the bakery closed for the day, the sisters sat at one of the tables, mugs of coffee forgotten while they reviewed their finances and considered what kind of offer they might be able to make. After an hour of debating and hesitation, they finally had their answer.

"Should we call Erika?" Carly asked.

"I think we should go over to the real estate office in person," Jill said. "Becca, do you want to do the honors?"

Becca wanted nothing more than to go home and take a hot bath, put on her comfiest pajamas, and forget this day—and yesterday—ever happened. Instead, she nodded. An offer was being made, her sisters were in agreement, and this was a little exciting, if not a bit scary.

She saw the apprehension in their eyes, too.

"I'll go," she said with a nod. And then she'd go home and tear open a pint of chocolate ice cream, where hopefully she could zone out in front of the television for a couple of hours. Most days after working at the bakery, all she could think about was getting off her feet and sleeping, but today all she could think about was Jonah.

Not the good parts, like the time he'd won her a pink stuffed bear at the carnival, which she'd kept on her bed right up until the day that they broke up, or the hopeful look in his eyes right before he slid down onto one knee and reached into his pocket for his grandmother's ring. No, all she could think about was how betrayed she'd felt the day he'd told her he was moving, realizing that his mind was made up, that he was going with or without her. How the person she'd trusted, and shared her dreams with, had broken more than their relationship, he'd also made her doubt every good memory, the parts that had made her feel loved.

"I'm excited!" Carly said now, looking at her eagerly.

Becca pulled her thoughts back to the present. "I am too. A little."

Not at the prospect of seeing Jonah, though.

And, if all went well and they won the bid, maybe she wouldn't have to. There'd be nothing left to keep him in town.

Her heart hurt a little at that thought, thinking of how she hadn't been enough for him, but then she knew that he could have made the same argument—and he did. She'd put the bakery over him.

And she was doing it all over again.

The sun was still warm and high in the sky when she stepped outside, but even though she'd made the same short walk just yesterday, everything felt different today. Her eyes darted from Concetti's Pizzeria to the flower shop across the street, looking for any sign of Jonah, who might be at the market on the corner right now, or in the window of the bookstore up ahead.

She didn't even realize she'd been holding her breath until she let it out the moment the door to the real estate office closed behind her. The lobby was mercifully empty, and after hearing the jingle of the door, Erika poked her head around her door.

"Becca! I was going to call over to the bakery before I left for the day to see if you and your sisters had made a decision."

Becca squared her shoulders and said proudly, "We have."

They hadn't even discussed it yet with Nana, but that was a good thing, wasn't it? Nana would approve, just like she'd approved of all the small and not-so-small changes the sisters had made to the bakery in recent months. She had embraced her new stage of life, and she made it clear that she wanted the girls to do the same. To make the bakery their own.

Becca held out the offer that Jill had typed up and Erika read it without giving away a reaction.

When Becca didn't think she could wait much longer, she worked up the nerve to say, "Is it enough? To outbid Jonah?"

"Oh. About that." Erika set the paper on the front desk and gave a little grimace. "The offer isn't just about money."

Becca blinked. "I'm not following."

"Denise has a lot of attachment to the space. That dress shop was in her family for generations. She wants to make sure it falls into the right hands."

Becca nodded, feeling more confident. Denise wasn't just a regular patron of the bakery, she had also become a friend when Becca needed one the most. She'd been kind and understanding that Becca's plans had changed, and instead of making it all about business, she'd insisted that Becca sit for a cup of tea. They didn't talk about Becca's heartache that day; Denise could see that Becca wasn't ready. Instead, Denise had told Becca about her own romantic disappointment, about another wedding dress she'd designed that was also never worn, but instead hung in the closet, waiting, hoping, for the right man to come along.

Becca felt sad to think that it hadn't happened for Denise. Would the same be said for her? Considering she hadn't made time to date in years, it was all too possible.

"Surely she'd be thrilled to hear that another multi-generational business wants the space," Becca said, feeling better about her prospects. "Denise has always been a loyal customer at the bakery."

But to her surprise, all Erika did was give a little tip of her head. "I'll pass on both offers to her, but I'm afraid the decision lies with her."

Becca nodded again. "Okay, then. Well, thank you."

"Thank you!" Erika said, then, before Becca could turn and walk out the door, she added: "Good luck."

Becca felt her earlier excitement begin to wane. She thought she didn't need luck, but something in Erika's face told her that she just might, and that it had nothing to do with Denise and everything to do with her ex-fiancé.

If there was one thing that Becca knew about Denise, it was that her favorite treat from the bakery was a caramel fudge brownie, something she only ordered when she had time to sit and enjoy one with a cup of coffee, because the bridal shop had a strict no food policy that even Denise had honored.

The other thing that Becca knew about Denise was that she had looked as crestfallen as Becca felt when Becca told her that her engagement was called off and that she wouldn't be needing her custom-designed dress after all. They'd spent weeks together, first brainstorming the design, then tweaking the fit, and sharing in the excitement when it was finally finished.

Unlike the rest of the town, it wasn't just pity that had shown in Denise's eyes when Becca had told her one afternoon, while plating a caramel brownie, that Jonah had moved away—and on with his life. It was heartache. That conversation might have been years ago, but Becca still remembered it clearly, how it hit her square in the chest, reminding her that this town was full of people who genuinely cared about her, and who knew her story. It had reaffirmed her decision to stay right here, where she belonged.

The bakery was always closed to the public on Wednesdays, but that didn't mean Becca necessarily stopped baking. With a box of caramel brownies carefully placed in the basket of her bicycle the next morning, Becca pedaled to Denise's cottage—a sweet, yellow-painted house with a cheerful front porch not far from the center of town.

She parked the old cruiser against a sturdy tree trunk and

took the steps quickly. But she stopped short of knocking on the red front door when she heard a rumble of laughter coming from inside.

Denise had company.

Becca dropped her hand, deciding between trying again in a few hours or leaving the box of brownies on the doormat when she heard the laughter again, louder this time.

She gripped the pastry box tighter. She knew that laugh, even if it had been a long time since it last graced her ears.

Denise had company all right. But Becca no longer had any hesitation about interrupting.

She turned back to the door and knocked again, firmly, making sure that she was heard.

A moment later, the door slowly opened to Denise's surprised face, which folded into one of delight when she saw the box that Becca was holding.

"Good morning, Denise," Becca said pleasantly, her gaze flicking over the woman's shoulder to the front living room, where from this angle she could only make out a man's shoe. "I just whipped up a batch of these caramel brownies this morning and I immediately thought of you. We haven't seen you in the bakery lately!"

"Oh, I know." Denise tutted. "Ever since I decided to retire, I haven't had an easy excuse to pop over."

"I was so sorry to hear about your shop," Becca said, thinking how Nana's choice to step away from the bakery came easier knowing that her granddaughters would take care of it.

And fight for it.

Gathering her courage, Becca said, "I suppose you've

heard from Erika that my sisters and I have made an offer on the space? It would be the ideal way to expand the bakery."

She gave what she could only hope was a convincing smile.

"I couldn't agree more!" Denise said. "When I heard that the Sunshine Sisters had made an offer, it warmed my heart! It was such a difficult decision to close my business, as you can imagine. I've been running it for over forty years!"

Becca gave a nod of understanding. She knew all too well that even the thought of walking away from a family business felt like losing a second home.

Denise skirted her eyes to the side and then leaned in to whisper, "I feel compelled to tell you that Jonah is here."

Of course he was.

"I'm aware that he's back in town. Don't worry about my feelings," she assured Denise. "The breakup was a long time ago."

Denise studied her for a moment and then gave her a kind smile.

"Well then, why don't you come in and have a brownie with me?" Denise said brightly. "I just put on a pot of tea. Can you believe that I often go for weeks without having a visitor and today I have two?"

Becca certainly could.

She stepped inside the house and turned into the open entranceway to the living room where Jonah was perched on a wingback armchair, looking almost as uncomfortable at the sight of her as he was sitting on the loud, floral fabric.

"Jonah. Three times in three days, isn't that something?"

"And isn't it wonderful to have the two of you here, together again?" Denise exclaimed.

Becca's smile was frozen as she looked down at the coffee table, where two plates of eggs Benedict were half-eaten.

"Look, Jonah! Becca brought these delicious brownies." She turned to Becca, motioning for her to sit on the rocking chair. "And Jonah stopped by with these amazing crabcakes that he turned into an extraordinary breakfast for us. You plan to put these on the menu of your new restaurant?"

Jonah nodded, looking proud as he relaxed at the mention of his food. "But they're not just any crabcakes. I've tweaked that recipe for four years."

Meaning that he'd continued to tweak it after he'd claimed to have perfected it shortly before he'd hightailed it out of town. Becca managed to stifle her sigh.

"Oh!" Denise said. "The kettle's whistling. Sugar?"

Becca nodded. "Please."

She watched as Denise disappeared down the hall and was safely out of earshot before turning to Jonah and hissing, "Crabcakes eggs Benedict?"

"Like I couldn't say the same to you. Brownies?"

"At least I didn't take over her kitchen." Becca lifted her chin a notch. "Besides, the brownies happen to be her favorite and I haven't seen her in the bakery recently. You may recall that in addition to running a store next door, Denise designed my wedding dress?"

That silenced him.

"I wasn't aware that you even knew Denise," Becca added.

"Now that I'm back in town, there's more reason to get

to know everyone in the community." Jonah raised an eyebrow. "I'm sure as a business owner you're aware of how important it is to know your customers."

Only Denise was hardly a customer. She was the gatekeeper.

"Why don't you try a bite?" Jonah lifted his plate and extended it to her.

Becca had to admit that it looked as good as it smelled, not that she was surprised. Jonah loved to cook as much as she enjoyed baking. They'd spend hours tweaking recipes, talking about food trends, and she was always the first opinion he sought when he made a new dish.

Back then, he'd watch her carefully, eager for her approval.

Somehow, she thought she saw the same question in his eyes now.

She pursed her lips, about to say no when her stomach betrayed her, grumbling so loudly that her cheeks flushed.

Jonah tossed his head back, laughing so loudly that Becca couldn't help but smile.

She'd missed that laugh. She'd missed a lot of things about Jonah.

"I hear laughter!" Denise shuffled back into the room with a tea tray. She gave a hopeful look at Becca, and Becca hated to disappoint the woman.

Especially when she was the sole decision-maker when it came to who would get her storefront.

"Jonah was trying to convince me to try his dish," she said.

"Oh, it's delicious!" Denise cooed, causing a little smirk to lift the corner of Jonah's mouth.

Becca narrowed her eyes slightly at him and then picked up the fork. "I'm sure it is. Jonah was always a wonderful chef."

She forked off a piece of the crabcake, covered in a runny egg and a sauce that she was certain Jonah had spent weeks perfecting.

She chewed thoughtfully, all too aware of Jonah's eyes on her.

"Delicious," she said, almost disappointed by the fact, even though she hadn't doubted him for a second.

Jonah was talented. He deserved his own restaurant. Just not here. Not now.

"And now for dessert!" Denise laughed. "My, what a feast on a weekday! Jonah, there's enough for us all." She held the bakery box out to him, and after a brief hesitation, he plucked one free.

Becca took the opportunity to observe him, tasting the brownie, chewing it, knowing that he'd eaten it before, because it was one of their older recipes, passed down from Nana.

"Tastes good, doesn't it?" Denise remarked, taking a second bite of her own.

Jonah gave a little nod as his gaze swung to Becca. "It tastes like home."

She stared at him for a moment, her mouth dry, and when she reached for her teacup, her hands were shaking.

"So, as much as I'm enjoying this visit, I'm sure there's

no avoiding the elephant in the room." Denise looked at each of them. "You both want the space."

Jonah darted his gaze to Becca as she set down her tea, giving Denise her full attention.

"A new restaurant in town is about as exciting as the thought of a larger bakery!" Denise sighed. "It's important to me that the space be used for something...meaningful. Something that will bring joy to the community."

"Well, if there's one place in town that knows how to bring people joy, it's the bakery," Becca said with confidence.

"Yes, but the bakery already has a way to serve people," Jonah said.

Becca narrowed her eyes at him but he didn't stop.

"You have a newly renovated shop," he pointed out. Then, to Denise: "Have you seen what a lovely transformation they've done with the bakery?"

Flattery wasn't going to get him anywhere.

Denise nodded. "It's lovely. Just lovely."

Becca gave a tight smile. "Thank you. So you can just imagine what we could do with more space. With more chairs and tables, we could seat more customers. The bakery has always been a gathering place for people here in Hope Hollow."

Take that, Jonah.

Sure enough, a pinch appeared between his eyebrows.

"And that's exactly how I envision my restaurant. It wouldn't just be a place to grab a quick dinner, it would be a place where special moments would be celebrated. Birthdays. Anniversaries."

He stopped abruptly. Becca wondered if he'd been about to say engagements.

"Oh, you both do raise strong points." Denise bit nervously on her lip. "I'm afraid I'm going to need some time to think this over."

"Of course," Becca and Jonah said in unison.

She glanced at him then away. Even now, looking straight into his eyes hurt too much, reminding her of the connection they once shared.

"Take all the time you need," Becca said. They weren't in a rush, after all. But she fully intended to return again soon with another plate of brownies.

Jonah, however, looked like he wanted to say something and then stopped himself.

"Thank you for your time, Denise," he said as he stood. "It was good seeing you again."

"And good seeing you two!" Denise gushed as she walked them to the door. "Especially together."

For a moment, Becca wondered if Jonah might lead this poor woman to believe they were reunited just to lock in the space. Considering that he'd shown up uninvited with grocery bags and convinced this woman to let him personally prepare her breakfast, she wouldn't put anything past him.

"Seeing Becca again is certainly one of the best things about being back in Hope Hollow," he said.

His gaze seemed to lock on hers, not in challenge, but in something else. For a moment, the fact that they were both here under selfish motives, both vying for the same thing, was forgotten, and in its place a hundred memories that they'd once shared seemed to connect them, leaving everything else to fall by the wayside.

It would be so easy to believe him, but that would require thinking that any of his promises had ever been anything other than empty words.

Becca swallowed hard. "Well, I should probably get back to my sisters."

She waited for Jonah to point out that the bakery was closed on Wednesdays. He managed to refrain, but the gleam in his eyes told her he saw through her excuse.

"And I should probably get back to my grandfather," Jonah said.

"And I should probably start thinking about what to do with the space." Denise tipped her head. "I'm sorry I couldn't give you a decision sooner. It's not just about the money to me, you see. It's about making sure that those four walls are filled with...heart."

Heart.

Heart was one thing that Jonah didn't have.

Jonah stood on Denise's front porch, probably just as aware as Becca that Denise was likely poking her head around a curtain at this very moment.

Becca said nothing as she walked down the steps, and he met her stride for stride, even though he hadn't a clue what to say—or maybe, where to begin. She pulled her bicycle from the tree it had been leaning against and began walking it onto the sidewalk.

"Bec," he started, once they'd reached the corner.

Her hazel eyes blazed when she stopped to look up at him. "Denise's house is out of earshot. We can stop pretending now."

"I'm not pretending," he said, affronted. He swallowed back the emotions building in his chest, grappling for where to start. "I meant what I said back there."

"Which part?" She shook her head. "Forget it. I already know what your words mean, Jonah. Nothing."

He wanted to say that wasn't fair, but maybe it was. Maybe it was just as foolish as him thinking that he could come back here, reclaim the life he'd left behind, and the dream he'd had. The one with her in it.

"Can we talk?" he asked softly.

She hesitated for a moment, and his pulse quickened, but all too quickly she shook her head, shooting down his hopes.

"I'm done arguing, Jonah."

"Who said anything about arguing?" he countered.

"Isn't that what we're doing right now?" She tossed up a hand. "Look, Jonah, I get it, okay. You're here, in town, and we're both after the same thing."

"And if we weren't?" he asked.

Her eyebrows shot up. "Why? Are you thinking of pulling your offer?"

So there it was. She didn't want to talk about them. Because there was no them, at least not to her. It was all about her wishes versus his.

Maybe, that's all it ever was.

"Look, I have to go," she said impatiently.

"The bakery is closed on Wednesdays," he reminded her.

Her eyes narrowed as she climbed onto her bicycle seat. "Believe it or not, I have more going on in my life than just the bakery."

Jonah once again watched as Becca hurried away from him, when once it had been toward him.

Well, that hadn't gone as planned.

He kept his own pace slow as he walked toward Main Street, knowing that now probably wasn't the best time to try and have another chat with Becca, not when, once again in his life, nothing was going as planned. Yesterday he'd hoped to start over, keep things nice, maybe even show that he still cared about her. Heck, he'd even considered rescinding his offer, letting her have the space next door, until he saw the bakery. The changes she'd made to it. The way she was so at peace there. The way she'd been happy with her choice to stay back instead of join him on the West Coast.

Unlike him, she hadn't regretted her decision one bit.

And now, the only hope he had of staying here, making a life for himself in Hope Hollow, was to build a new restaurant. And right now, the only chance he had of doing that was in the space next door to the bakery.

"Jonah!"

He glanced across the street as he slowed at the intersection. There, quickly approaching, was Nick Sutton. They'd gone to school in the same grade as Becca, and always gotten along. After a short-lived marriage, Nick had returned to town with his daughter about a year before Jonah decided to move out west.

If anyone understood the complicated feelings that came with returning home again, it was Nick.

"I heard you were back!" Nick grinned and pulled him in for a bear hug, giving him a slap on the back. "It's good to see you, man."

"It's good to be back."

And it was. How many days had he shown up to work in that kitchen, wishing that he had stayed true to his dream? How many evenings had he cooked someone else's recipes instead of the ones he'd planned to create?

How many nights had he returned to an empty and quiet apartment, exhausted but unable to sleep, thinking of how he'd once spent this time with Becca?

Nick had been a good friend to him growing up, and even though they hadn't kept in touch while Jonah was in LA, Nick's return to town had proved that they had a way of picking things up right where they left off.

If only Becca could have done the same. But then, even he knew not to dream that big.

"You back to stay?"

"That's the plan." Jonah caught the irony in his words. "I'm hoping to open a restaurant. I put a bid on the old wedding dress shop."

"The town needs some variety!" Nick said enthusiastically.

"Well, don't get too excited," Jonah warned. "My offer hasn't been accepted. I'm afraid that I've run into some competition."

"Another restauranteur?" Nick looked confused. This was a small town and not many new people moved in, only passed through. Hope Hollow was built on generations of families who stayed and never left.

Or, like him, left and returned.

"Actually, the bakery is thinking of expanding."

Nick's eyes widened. "I'm surprised that Carly didn't tell me!"

Now it was Jonah's turn to be confused. "I saw Carly in the bakery yesterday but I didn't realize you were on good terms." He also hadn't realized Carly was back in town at all. Things had changed in his short absence, he realized.

People too.

"More than that," Nick said with a grin. "We're back together."

Back together. Jonah let that sink in, wondering if the same could be possible for him and Becca.

He'd hoped so. Now, he didn't see how.

"Knowing Carly, she didn't want to jinx things," Jonah said, thinking of Becca's kid sister and her endless optimism.

"Probably," Nick agreed. He peered at Jonah, unable to fight the amusement on his face. "But you and Becca? Head to head?" He gave a little laugh. "Sorry, man. I know it's not funny."

No. It wasn't.

"Except...you and Becca." Nick whistled. "How's that going?"

There was no that or them. Except that somehow, there still was. History had a way of bonding people, even when you tried to outrun the past.

"Not great," Jonah admitted. In fact, worse than he'd feared. He'd known that there was no guarantee that he and

Becca would find a way back together, even though he'd hoped for it, was prepared to fight for it, prove to her that he still cared. That he'd never stopped.

But losing out on his new restaurant was never something he'd considered.

"Sounds like you could use a night out," Nick suggested. "A couple of the guys are going out for drinks Saturday if you're interested."

Jonah nodded. "Count me in."

He could use some guy time.

Especially since the only girl he cared to spend any time with couldn't get away from him fast enough.

five

Now that Carly was back in town and living at Nana's, Becca and Jill made a point of gathering at the house for a family dinner each week, usually on Fridays.

"Is Carly bringing Nick tonight?" Jill asked on their walk across town.

Becca nodded. "I think Daisy's at a sleepover, though."

Jill motioned to the light up ahead, about to turn red, then looked at Becca squarely. "Makes our excuse about not having time for a relationship pretty moot, doesn't it?"

"Is there anyone in Hope Hollow you have your eye on?" Becca asked her sister, eager to keep the conversation—and her mind—off of her own personal life.

Jill hesitated just long enough to make Becca wonder if there actually was someone that her sister was interested in romantically, but before she could ask, they turned onto Nana's street, where, at the house next door, Jonah's old black Jeep was sitting in the driveway.

Becca groaned, wishing she could turn and walk away now, or hide behind a hedge.

"That Jonah's car?" Jill, of course, knew that it was. "Want me to let the air out of his tires?"

"Jill!" Becca gave her sister a playful swat, but the earlier stress she felt was replaced with laughter. Jill's mission, she supposed.

"Don't worry," Jill said, because no doubt she knew that Becca would be at least a little anxious. "The odds of him looking out the window right now are pretty slim."

True. And Becca would have to get used to seeing him around town, too.

Still, she picked up the pace until they were safely outside Nan's front door. Even though neither of them had lived here for several years, they let themselves in without knocking. It had been home since their father left, not long after Carly had been born, and their mother moved them all in with her mother, by then a widow. The five women had lived happily under this roof for years, and even now, long after Becca's mother had died from cancer when Becca was just a teenager, Becca still felt her presence. Carly was living here now with Nana, and their grandmother insisted they always call this house their home.

"We're back here!" Carly called out to them from the kitchen no sooner than they stepped into the front hall.

Like there was anywhere else they would be. The bright sunny kitchen was the hub of the home, the place where they gathered over the years more than any other room in the house. Where birthday cakes were frosted and the candles lit, where long chats over warm mugs of tea were had. It was a place of comfort, a place where Becca could never feel alone or anything but loved.

But today, Becca stopped short of crossing the threshold. There, on the counter, was a beautifully decorated cake that most certainly hadn't been picked up in the bakery today.

And standing not far behind it was Jonah.

She felt Jill's fingers press into her back, inching her forward as everyone seemed to stop what they were doing to stare at her. Carly, who might have found an excuse to text or hurry out into the hallway and urge her away, looked like she might not blink again.

Jonah's gaze was shifty, flitting from his grandfather to Becca and to the floor. Nick shifted awkwardly on his feet. Mr. Quincy stared at the cake.

And the only person in the entire room who was smiling was Nana.

Becca inwardly rolled her eyes. Of course. Jonah was back in town. And Nana saw an opportunity to play matchmaker. It wouldn't be the first time, considering she'd invited Nick to a family dinner not so long ago. Now that her work with Carly was complete, it would seem she'd set her sights on Becca.

"Becca! Look who's here!" Nana smiled widely, but her eyes were sharp.

Was tonight meant to be a surprise? It felt more like an ambush.

"Yes, Jonah and I have run into each other a few times since he's been back in town." But the last place she expected to see him was here, in her childhood home. Did the man have no sense of boundaries?

"So Jonah was just saying." From Nana's pleased tone, it was clear that Jonah hadn't shared many details.

"What are we celebrating?" Becca managed to ask as they approached the kitchen island, Jill close at her side.

If her Nana dared to say they were gathered here for Jonah's return she might just have to take this beautiful cake and shove it right in Jonah's face.

But instead, her grandmother gave a mysterious smile and said, "Does there ever have to be a reason for dessert?"

It was a line she used many times at the bakery, back when she spent her early mornings in the kitchen and the remainder of the day standing behind the counter, serving customers.

Becca wasn't one to argue with her grandmother, especially in this case, but a cake as exquisite as this one was rarely eaten without a specific purpose.

She cast a suspicious glance at Carly. Had Nick proposed? They hadn't been reunited for long, but then, lately, it seemed that anything was possible.

Her gaze went to Jonah. Well, almost anything.

"Did you make this?" Jill asked Carly.

"Nana did," Carly told her.

Jill tutted. She was the most protective of their grandmother and the arthritis that eventually forced her to leave the bakery and retire.

But Nana just waved away Jill's concern and said, "It's a beautiful night. Why don't you young ones start setting up outside."

Jonah came around the counter, catching Becca's eye in

the process, but she looked away and focused on the door. Escape.

Somehow, they got there at the same time, and Jonah, gallantly, stopped and held out an arm. Becca resisted the urge to insist he go through first if only so she could close the door behind him and run in the other direction. But eyes were watching, and so, heaving a long sigh, she played along.

No sooner had she stepped outside than she heard her grandmother say, "Oh, Jill, be a dear and help with the side dishes on the stove. And Carly, I need your help with the bread. Nick, why don't you find us more chairs?"

The door closed firmly behind Jonah. If Becca didn't know better, she might even think that her grandmother had turned the lock.

It had been a trap. And they'd both fallen for it.

Becca looked back at the house, where Nana's face was visible through the window over the kitchen sink just before it quickly disappeared again.

"I see my grandmother is happy to have you back in town," Becca commented.

"Happier than your sisters," Jonah remarked. He gave a little smile. "She's probably just happy that my grandfather is in good spirits."

Becca nodded. "I heard about his dog. Nana said he was pretty lonely. I'm sure it helps to have you there."

"Oh, I think your grandmother keeps him pretty occupied." Jonah met her eyes and for a moment, the animosity between them was gone, replaced by understanding.

"So," Becca said, taking a step back, needing to tear herself from that gaze, from any hint of connection they still shared. It was so much easier to stay mad at Jonah than to remember what she had once loved about him.

"So... How long do you think it will be before the others join us?" Jonah asked, giving her a conspiratorial look.

Oh, no. She wasn't about to fall back onto old times, act like nothing was wrong, or that they could just pick up where they left off. Too much had happened between them. Too much had been said.

And left unsaid.

"Knowing my grandmother? All night." But Becca knew that Carly and Jill would come to her rescue soon.

"Just so you know, when my grandfather told me we were having dinner with your grandmother, I didn't know you would be here," Jonah volunteered.

She looked at him squarely. "So sorry to disappoint you."

"I didn't mean it that way," he said, raising his voice to prove his point.

Becca held up a hand. "I'm not here to argue. I thought I was here to have a nice dinner with my family."

She stopped on that word. It wasn't lost on her that, if things had gone as planned, right now, Jonah would be her family.

She wondered if he thought about that too.

"And I'm not in town to make trouble. Honestly," he added, giving her a long look.

She stared at him, knowing he was telling the truth even without taking in the sincerity in his deep-set eyes. Just like she knew that he'd never set out to hurt her when he took the opportunity in LA.

How could he have been actively seeking to hurt her when he hadn't even been thinking of her at all?

"And I'm not looking for problems," she said, meeting him halfway. "All I want is to go about my life, quietly."

"That's all we both ever wanted," he said.

She raised an eyebrow. "It's what you once wanted. And then decided you didn't want it anymore. Along with me."

She didn't intend for her tone to sound so bitter, but it was out now, and she realized that her heart was starting to pound. Her eyes flicked to the kitchen window. Why weren't her sisters out here yet?

"I didn't stop wanting you," Jonah said, his voice low, his gaze unwavering in their hold on hers.

Becca swallowed hard against the pounding of her heart and then shook away the building emotions. He wasn't talking about now. He was talking about then—two years ago.

"I wanted you to come with me. I *asked* you to come with me," he reminded her.

She felt the same old argument they'd had then brewing to the surface now. "And leave behind everything that mattered to me?"

"I thought I mattered to you," he countered.

She opened her mouth and then closed it. "Forget it. We're just going down a road we've already traveled, Jonah. Decisions were made. Actions were taken. That was a long time ago."

Even though it didn't feel like it. Her days were routine, sliding into weeks and months. And just like that, two years had slipped by and absolutely nothing in her life had really changed.

Finally, she heard the back door open and Carly burst out, Jill close behind her. They each held a tray of food that they set on the table, and Becca was all too happy when each of them took a chair flanking the one she pulled out.

Jonah slowly sank into the chair across from Becca, turning his attention to his grandfather, who was leading Nana out of the house, along with Nick, managing two more chairs. Jill and Carly each gave Jonah an icy glare, but Nick seemed to give Jonah a look of solidarity before setting his chair beside Carly. For a moment, they were all quiet as the food was passed and praise was given to Nana for making the meal.

"We didn't just gather you here for a family dinner," Nana said, giving them all a coy smile. "The truth is, we have some news to share."

News? We? Becca couldn't imagine where this was going.

"I'll cut right to the point," Mr. Quincy said. "I've asked Sharon to marry me and she's accepted!"

Nana thrust a hand out, showing off a large diamond ring on her bony finger, and other than the sound of a faraway lawnmower, there wasn't a sound to be heard.

"*Married*?" Jill finally broke the silence, her eyes so wide that Becca might have laughed if she wasn't so stunned. "But you've only just started dating!"

"But Robert and I have known each other for decades!" Nana replied.

Jill slanted a glance at Becca. Had Nana forgotten that

she'd turned away her neighbor's advances for years before finally agreeing to give him a chance?

"And we're not exactly young," Robert pointed out. "I spent a lot of years chasing this woman. I wasn't about to let her get away too quickly."

"And I wasted a lot of years turning him down," Nana said, giving him a look of such loving regret that Becca almost felt herself tearing up—until she caught Jonah's eyes. Gone was any hint of amusement in his mouth, which was pulled in a tight, thin line.

Robert took Nana's hand and patted it. "We don't see any reason to let one more day pass us by."

Becca pulled in a breath and turned to Jill, who now looked resigned if not exactly pleased. Carly, however, stood and flung her arms around her grandmother.

"Congratulations, you two," she said, sounding like she meant it.

"Yes, of course, congratulations," Jonah said, seeming to finally find his voice.

Jill muttered her good wishes, followed by Nick, and then Becca, who couldn't match her younger sister's enthusiasm. It wasn't complicated for her, not like Becca. Or Jonah. Or Jill, who tended to like things just as they always were.

"That certainly explains the cake," Jill muttered.

"Oh, the cake! Let's bring it out now," Nana suggested.

"But we haven't eaten dinner yet," Jonah said, frowning no doubt about more than eating their courses out of order.

A twinkle appeared in Nana's eye. "Didn't you just hear what your grandfather said? Life is too short to push off the best parts."

"In that case, I'll do the honors," Nick said, rising to his feet. From the pace of his stride, Becca suspected that he was more eager to get away from the family drama than he was to taste the cake.

Becca half expected him to dash out to the driveway and peel out off down the street, or come back to the table with a handy excuse about Daisy, and a need to leave soon. Maybe Carly would go with him—Becca wouldn't blame her.

The silence stretched as Nana smiled and admired her ring, and Nick returned, with the cake and a bottle of champagne that he said he found chilling in the fridge.

"I hope I didn't overstep," he said, setting everything on the table.

"Nonsense! You saved me the trip," Nana said.

It was only then that Becca noticed the champagne flutes beside their wine glasses.

Robert Quincy did the honors of popping the cork and giving them each a bit of fizz. "A toast," he said, raising his glass. "To family!"

Family. Becca clinked her glass but when she tried to take a sip, it didn't go down easily.

She and Jonah were now forever linked, through their grandparents, and even though this wasn't the way it had been planned, dreamed, or expected, somehow, in the end, after everything, they would still become...family.

"So, Grandpa," Jonah said after the cake had been cut. The dinner was growing cold, but no one seemed very concerned about it—other than maybe Nick, whose eyes kept flitting back to the large bowl of pasta. "When's the big day?"

"Oh, it won't be a big day," Nana Parker explained.

Everyone in town under the age of sixty called her that and she loved it. Jonah still had fond memories of her handing him a cookie over the bakery counter and correcting his use of Mrs. Parker. She was Nana to everyone. But for a while, she'd felt like a true grandmother to him.

"More like a small celebration with our closest friends and family," Jonah's grandfather added.

"But everyone in town loves you, Nana!" Carly pointed out. Then, lowering her voice, she added, "Well, other than Frannie James."

They all slid their eyes to the hedge dividing the two women's properties. It was no secret that these neighbors had never been fond of each other, but Nana Parker surprised Jonah when she said, "Oh, and now she has one more reason not to like me. I've stolen Robert's affections from her."

Jonah stared at his grandfather. Since when had he become a ladies' man?

His grandfather chuckled away his embarrassment and said, "I was running out of ways to get Sharon's attention. Jealousy did the trick."

They all laughed, even Becca, Jonah noticed, but she stopped when her eyes locked with his.

"So when is the big day?" Carly asked.

"We were thinking two weeks or so," Robert said.

"Two *weeks*?" Becca spoke at the same time as Jonah, but when he tried to catch her eye again she looked away.

Jill's mouth seemed to have slackened, and only Carly was perfectly content, happily eating her food.

"As we said, we don't want to waste any more time." Nana gave an innocent blink, oblivious to Jill's shock. "I'll need a dress first. I saved the gown from my first wedding but it wouldn't feel right to wear it for this occasion. This is the start of the next chapter of my life and...it's important to have a new dress to mark that."

"I can go shopping with you if you'd like, Nana," Carly offered eagerly. "Daisy would love to come along." She and Nick exchanged a smile.

Jonah felt something in his gut twist. It was the look, the connection, one that he used to share and now no longer did. The ability to be in a room full of people and to know that there was one special person who was on your team most of all.

He looked up, feeling Becca's eyes on him now. She looked away just as quickly.

"Well, Denise did overhear Maria Concetti and me talking this morning at the market. She offered to make my dress, even though she closed her shop." Nana Parker shook her head. "She made sure to tell me what an honor it is to her that her last gown will be for me. Of course, I'm sure she's just saying that."

"Like how Maria offered to host a reception?" Jonah's grandfather winked.

"I highly doubt that any of your friends are just saying that to be polite!" Becca said. "You worked side by side for years, and everyone, especially Denise and Maria, knows that you—and the bakery—are pillars of the community."

She gave a little smile before sliding her gaze to him.

Jonah bit back his frustration because, of course, it was true. The bakery was as beloved as Nana Parker herself, and Denise wasn't immune to either's charms.

Meaning, he'd just have to find a few of his own.

"Why don't you let me help with some of the wedding plans?" The words were out of his mouth before he'd had time to give them proper thought. He didn't know anything about planning a wedding—Becca had handled most of that, and happily.

His grandfather gave him a grateful smile. "You'd do that?"

"Of course," Jonah said. "You're the only family I have."

"For now," he heard Becca grumble across the table.

"I'm sure that my mother would love to play piano at the ceremony," Nick volunteered.

"And I'm happy to do whatever I can to make this a special day for you both," Jonah said to his grandfather. Especially if it gave him an excuse to get to know Denise a little better in the process. If she was working on the gown, she'd be close to the wedding planning. And he knew an opportunity when he saw one.

Even if they didn't always go as planned.

Now, he saw Becca sit up a little straighter. "Oh, but it's tradition for the bride to plan the wedding. Surely, you haven't forgotten that much about wedding planning in just two years, Jonah?"

There was a moment of silence, interrupted only by Nana's gracious smile. "I think it's wonderful that you two both want to help. Truth be told, I was happy with something small, even at the town hall...but when Denise started telling me about the dress ideas she had, I'll admit that it was hard not to get swept away."

"Then you'll need a wedding as beautiful as your dress," Becca said firmly. "Something that shows...heart. Something that shows...commitment."

"I think we all want the same thing for these two love-birds," Jonah said lightly.

Becca's mouth pinched. "I think we do."

"Then it's settled. We'll have the most beautiful wedding that Hope Hollow has ever seen, all thanks to the two of you. Oh, I can't wait to tell Denise. She'll be so happy to know!" Nana Parker said.

Yes, Jonah suspected that Denise would be happy to hear this news.

But as for Becca, she looked about as unhappy as he was starting to feel.

"I don't know what's more unbelievable," Becca said once she and Jill arrived back at the cottage they shared—more like the one that Jill was kind enough to let Becca move into when her engagement ended. "That Nana is getting remarried or that she's marrying Jonah's grandfather."

The walk from dinner had been one of silence, comfortable enough since the sisters were used to each other's company, but Becca knew that they were each working through their own opinions and feelings.

Nana was one of the most independent people that

Becca had ever known; well, with the exception of Jill. She'd only turned down poor Mr. Quincy's advances for at least the past decade. Once, Becca and Jonah used to laugh about it.

Now, there was nothing funny about this situation.

"You'll believe it when the invitations show up. Didn't you hear what Nana said before we left? She's going to spend tonight putting together the guest list and ordering the invitations. Express." Jill shook her head, sharing Becca's disbelief. "I bet half of the town will show up!"

"For sure they'll reach maximum capacity at Concetti's," Becca agreed.

"Good thing Frankie Concetti is a volunteer firefighter. Maybe he'll overlook the code this once." Jill managed to laugh, and eventually, Becca did too.

"I'm happy for her," Becca said, dropping onto the sofa in the living room and hugging one of many throw pillows to her chest. For so long, Nana had been alone, even though she claimed that was impossible with three granddaughters, especially when they had tried her patience in their teenage years.

"You certainly seemed supportive." Jill raised an eyebrow as she sat down on the armchair she preferred. "Offering to help with the wedding preparations?"

"I wasn't about to let Jonah take all the glory!" Becca cried. "How presumptuous was that?"

Jill hesitated. "It was sort of sweet."

"Sweet?" Becca shook her head. "Since when are you giving Jonah a pass?"

"I'm not," Jill said firmly. "What he did to you was

unforgivable. But you have to admit that was a nice gesture on his part."

Becca harrumphed. "Let's just see if he's still in town when the wedding comes around."

"I take it you haven't heard any more from Denise about her decision?" Jill knew all about the run-in that Becca had had with Jonah at Denise's house, and Carly did too. Both had agreed that it gave them an edge. Their brownies beat the legs off Jonah's crabs any day.

"It's only been a few days and she said she needed some time to think about it, but something tells me that this wedding will sway her decision, and hopefully in our favor," Becca remarked.

"Becca." Jill's tone was one of warning. "You didn't volunteer to help with Nana's weddings in order to curry favor with Denise, did you?"

"Of course not!" Becca cried but then let her shoulders drop. "Well, maybe a little. But only because I know that's why Jonah offered. He saw an opportunity. And Jonah is always one to take those, as we know."

Just thinking about it now made her blood boil. The man was determined to charm his way into that space next to the bakery, but he wouldn't charm his way back into her good graces. Not when she saw him for who he really was now.

"Yes, but now you've gotten yourself into a situation where you're going to have to plan the wedding with Jonah," Jill pointed out. "Did you stop to think of that?"

Becca groaned when she closed her eyes, trying to shut out the reality of the situation. They hadn't even spent much time planning their own wedding—she'd taken the reins and run with it, and Jonah was just happy to go along with what she wanted. He'd said the wedding wasn't important to him, that it was everything else that mattered.

At the time she'd seen that as sweet. Now, she knew that it meant he didn't care, at least not enough.

"No. I didn't stop to think about that." She sat up straighter, looking at her sister with hope. "Did you bring any of that cake home?"

Jill gave a small smile as she pushed off the chair. "I wish. It was delicious. Nana certainly has the touch."

"We learned from the best," Becca agreed.

"I'll get us some ice cream from our stash." Jill walked into the kitchen, which was the only room in the old house that had been renovated, and returned with two pints and two spoons. "Mint chip or chocolate?"

But her sister was already extending the chocolate ice cream before Becca could speak up. "This is what I love about Hope Hollow. You and me. Our favorite ice cream. If nothing ever changed, I would be fine with that."

Jill peeled the lid off her pint and settled back on the couch. "But things do change, Becca. We never thought Nana would leave the bakery and she did. And we definitely never thought she'd accept one of Robert Quincy's overtures, and now she's getting married. We'll never again go over to her house and have a quiet holiday as just the four of us."

Becca frowned, thinking of that. "That's the part about change that I don't like. It always includes losing something."

"Or gaining something," Jill countered through a mouthful of ice cream. "It just depends on how you see it."

"What am I gaining out of this experience?" Becca asked.

"A new grandpa?" Jill teased.

"Stop!" Becca pleaded, but she was laughing now. Even though the thought of this new dynamic made her feel a little like crying. There would be no more long chats, just as women, in the kitchen. Christmas mornings wouldn't be spent eating cookies with their coffee in matching pajamas, while old holiday movies played in the background. Robert would bring new traditions to the house.

And worse, he might bring Jonah with him.

"We've made some other changes recently that weren't so bad. That's all I'm saying," Jill said.

"Something tells me we're back to talking about expanding the bakery," Becca replied. She tipped her head. "I thought you were only doing it to help me get back at Jonah."

"At first. But the more I think about it, it would be exciting. The changes we've already made have been such a success. Why stop now?"

Becca nodded. She had to agree that she felt the same. It was exciting to think of bringing the bakery into the next phase, making it bigger, and brighter, and serving more people. Maybe they could offer classes if they had the space. Gingerbread house events at the holidays, or chocolate workshops around Valentine's Day.

She dipped her spoon into her ice cream. She was getting ahead of herself. Dreaming again. And she knew all too well what happened when she did that.

Disappointment.

"So you still haven't said how you plan to handle working with Jonah on these wedding plans," Jill said, a little smile twisting her mouth.

"I'm glad you find this so amusing," Becca said dryly.

"It's not necessarily a bad thing, is it?" Jill asked. "For the two of you to get along? Considering the fact that you are going to be…step-grand-siblings? Or would it be more like…kissing cousins?"

"Gross!" Becca flung a throw pillow at her sister. "See, our two families were destined to be united, just not through us."

Now Jill's expression sobered. "Seriously, though, Becca. How are you holding up? It can't be easy having him back in town. The space next door aside, are you okay with this?"

Becca hesitated. Over the years, it had become easier to not think of Jonah. To not wonder what might have happened if he'd never left. Or if she'd gone with him.

"We both made our choices," Becca said now, speaking the same words she'd told herself so many times over the past two years. "We both did what was best for us."

"Us? Or one another?" Jill set down her ice cream. "Jonah didn't think of the two of you at all when he accepted that job in California."

Becca fell silent. "What Jonah and I had was always built around our careers."

And Sunrise Sisters Bakery was more than her career. It was her life. From the time she was a little girl baking with her mother to now, surrounded by her sisters. They might offer new treats and have different seating and light fixtures, but the heart of it remained. That was one thing she could always be sure of when everything else felt uncertain.

"Things worked out the way they were supposed to," she said confidently. "I have the life I wanted. A full one. Our bakery. My family. This town. What more could I really want?"

Jill didn't look convinced when Becca popped the lid back on her ice cream pint and walked into the kitchen to return it to the freezer. But she knew what her sister was thinking because it was the same thing that was on her mind.

The very thing that Carly had found. And now Nana.

Love.

Six

If Becca was going to plan Nana's wedding, then research was in order. On her break the next day, she hurried down Main Street to the town's only bookstore, a cozy little storefront now owned and operated by Joanna Newman, Carly's best friend since childhood.

Joanna was carrying a stack of paperbacks that nearly reached her chin when Becca pushed through the door.

"Let me help you with that!" Becca hurried to retrieve a few of the books from the top of the pile before they could all topple over.

"Thanks." Joanna grinned. "It's easier with hardbacks. Heavier, though."

Becca followed her to the display table where Joanna started arranging the books Becca recognized as their next book club selection. She picked one up, deciding that she should probably purchase it while she was here.

"Oh? You're actually going to read this one, are you?" Joanna noticed Becca skimming the back cover.

Becca blushed. "Guilty as charged. I always intend to read the books for book club."

"Which is exactly why I don't like that club even though I should. It does bring me business." Joanna shook her head. "They may as well call it happy hour instead of a book club at this rate."

Becca laughed. "Well, this time I have an honest to good excuse for not having the time. I'm wedding planning—"

Joanna straightened in surprise. "No! Really! Oh, I heard Jonah was back and I wasn't sure if I should bring him up, but..."

Before Becca could even process what Joanna was saying, she was being pulled in for a tight hug.

"No. No, you've misunderstood. My *grandmother's* getting married."

"Oh!" Joanna dropped her arms. "Well. I mean, that's a surprise too. Carly didn't tell me."

"We just found out last night," Becca said, managing not to shudder at the strange turn of events.

"So she's marrying..." Here Joanna paused to make the connection.

"Robert Quincy," Becca confirmed. "Jonah's grandfather." Then, catching the look of horror on her friend's face, she added, "I know."

"Wow." Joanna shook her head. "I mean...wow. Are you okay with this?"

"I am," Becca assured her. "My grandmother seems happier than I've seen her in years. And as for Jonah...." Just saying his name made her stomach tighten. "We're just...."

She couldn't finish that sentence. They weren't friends. They weren't anything, really.

When once, they'd been everything.

"I was actually here for some wedding planning books. Are they still near the back wall?"

Joanna gave her what Becca had come to know as "the look." Pity and sympathy and good intentions all rolled into one.

Becca laughed uneasily. "It's fine, really. Jonah and I are old news. I've been over him for like...years."

Joanna didn't look convinced but she nodded her head. "I haven't moved anything. And you may find some good titles on second weddings and later-in-life weddings, too."

The phone rang from the office. "Oh, that might about the shipment that's been delayed. If anyone comes to the counter, will you give me a shout?"

Becca nodded and then walked through the stacks of books to the back wall where sure enough the wedding books were on full display, just like the last time she'd gone looking for them, nearly three years ago, the day after Jonah had proposed. Only last time, she'd been an excited bride-to-be with a sparkling ring on her left hand and a heart full of anticipation.

She let her gaze slide right past the covers of glowing brides in lace ball gowns, eventually falling on the ones that Joanna had mentioned. She bent down to reach for one that was particularly fitting, showing a greying couple basking in confetti when the door jangled and she turned around to see none other than Jonah walk through the door, looking relaxed in jeans and a blue tee-shirt.

"Oh, for goodness sake!" Becca muttered and then quickly darted to the side, hoping that she would be able to stay out of sight in the—she looked up, stifling a groan—self-help section.

Jonah, who wasn't headed for the cookbook section as she'd assumed, marched straight to the wedding shelf, where Becca was clearly visible.

"Becca?" He looked surprised to see her until his gaze shifted up to the genre header and he gave her a funny look.

"It's not what you think," she insisted. "I'm here for the wedding books."

"Which are two shelves over," he pointed out, his mouth starting to twitch.

"Yes, well, sometimes books get misplaced." Becca pursed her lips and bent down, hoping to prove her point by finding a misshelved wedding book only to be face to face with a workbook that promised to help readers recover from breakups.

Jonah raised an eyebrow. "It appears we're here for the same reason then. Imagine that, you and me, once again after the same thing."

"We did both offer to help plan our grandparents' wedding," she said.

"If I remember correctly, I offered to help and *then* you offered." He gave her a little smile. "If I didn't know better, I'd say you were looking to spend a little time with me."

"Don't flatter yourself," she scoffed. But she couldn't stop her gaze from homing in on his chest and arms. Had he been working out more in California? He had. Definitely, he had.

Tearing her stare from his shiny new muscles, she said, "It's my grandmother's wedding. Of course I'm going to help. Besides, I know what I'm doing."

"And you think I don't?" Far from insulted, he seemed amused by their situation.

"Well, I was the one who did all of the planning for our wedding," she reminded him. There was no sense in adding that it had been a complete waste of her time. Now, she saw it as a good experience. She knew exactly what to bother with and what to skip.

And these books, she now thought, were probably worth skipping.

She turned to leave when the door jingled again and, to both her horror and delight, Denise walked into the bookstore.

"Denise!" Becca smiled at the woman, but her expression froze when she felt Jonah come to stand behind her. His presence was a warm reminder of the familiarity they once shared, pulling on all her senses and bringing her back to a place when this kind of proximity was comforting. She stiffened and moved subtly to the side, eager to create some distance.

"Denise!" he said, the smile evident in his voice.

"Look at you two! Here together!" Denise waggled her eyebrows as she scooted around a display table.

"We bumped into each other," Becca explained. Then, remembering what her grandmother had said yesterday, she added, "I hear you're making my grandmother's wedding dress?"

"Oh, isn't it exciting! I know I've closed my shop, but I

still have more fabric than I'll ever know what to do with. An entire room of my house is a cloud of tulle!"

"That sounds beautiful," Becca said with a sigh. When she was engaged, she loved leaving the bakery to go next door, surrounded by beautiful gowns and veils, and a reminder of everything she had to look forward to. Then, after Jonah left, she stopped walking by the storefront at all, the window displays served a new purpose and sparked a new emotion. One that showed everything she almost had but had lost instead.

"I couldn't resist sending off one more happy bride, especially your grandmother, Becca. Oh!" Denise's eyes popped when she looked at Jonah. "And your grandfather! Imagine that."

Yes, imagine that. Only it wasn't something that Becca had ever imagined. Sure, they'd teased Nana over the years, urging her to accept one of Robert Quincy's many dinner invitations, even if it was only for friendship. But this outcome?

Not even in the realm of possibility. Yet it was happening. Like so many things in life, she never could have planned for it.

"I'm helping my grandmother plan the wedding, so I'm sure I'll be joining her for all the dress fittings," Becca told Denise.

"We're *both* helping to plan," Jonah cut in.

"But...I thought your grandmother said something about the courthouse, something small..." Denise looked at Becca in confusion.

"It would seem that you making the dress inspired her to

have something a little more formal," Becca said, sensing that Denise was pleased by this news. "But they're still planning on getting married in two weeks, so we don't have much time."

"I know Maria offered to host the reception," Denise said eagerly. "Oh, it must mean so much to them both to have you two helping out."

Becca swallowed hard, wishing she could be happier about this union. It was both surprising and unexpected. She just needed time to let it sink in.

"It's important to me that the day is special," Becca said honestly.

"With your help, I'm sure it will be," Denise said.

Becca hesitated, knowing she could let the conversation stop there, but then decided that she may as well ask the question that she knew Jonah was also considering.

"Have you...given any more thought to our offers?" She felt her stomach tighten as she waited for the news.

"You know, with this dress to design, I've been a little distracted, especially with the turnaround time." Denise looked nearly as anxious as Becca felt.

Becca nodded. "Of course."

Jonah cleared his throat. "We don't want to rush you."

Didn't they, though? The sooner they knew the fate of the space, the sooner they could begin to move forward, separately.

Unless he opened his restaurant right next to the bakery, that was.

"I'm sure I'll have an answer by the wedding day, though," Denise promised. "Your grandmother's dress is my first priority at the moment, especially since I have only two weeks to complete it."

Two more weeks of waiting for an answer on the space? Meaning two more weeks for Jonah to think of a way to snatch it out from under her.

"There's a lot to consider," Denise continued. "And I know that you'd both do right by it in your own ways. I just...need to make sure that it goes to the person with the best intentions. Someone who isn't thinking of how they could benefit but how they could put a smile on the faces of the people of our town."

"Well, for the next two weeks I think we'll all be thinking about how to put a smile on the bride's and groom's faces," Jonah said, shifting closer to Becca.

She inched away, but Denise's eyes began to gleam in a way that made Becca a little nervous.

"Well, isn't that so? The two of you, going out of your way, to make sure your grandparents are happy." She tapped her nose and gave them a smile as she moved toward the newsstand, where the bridal magazines took center stage.

"What did she mean by that?" Jonah whispered once she was out of earshot.

"I think it means she'll be paying close attention to how we handle these wedding plans," Becca said thoughtfully.

Because Denise couldn't possibly think there could be any more to it than that, could she?

~

Rustic Tavern was about as old as Hope Hollow itself, but like many of the businesses in town, it survived through the generations. Some saw this as a good thing. For a long time, Jonah didn't. It stifled progress. Kept the new guys out.

It killed dreams. Some might say, it even killed spirits.

But tonight, the only spirits Jonah was thinking of were of the beverage variety. He pulled open the door and stepped inside the dimly lit room, feeling the weight of his shoulders lift when Nick held up a hand from across the bar.

Jonah crossed the room quickly, or as quickly as he could, given that half the people there stopped to greet him, pat him on the back, ask him how long he was in town for, and how things were going in Seattle, was it? Or San Diego?

He didn't bother to correct these old neighbors and classmates any more than he wanted to answer their other questions. They were just being friendly, he knew. Maybe a little curious, but then that's how life was here in Hope Hollow. Everyone knew everyone.

And most of these people probably had opinions on his breakup with Becca.

Finally, after several polite excuses, he managed to make his way to the back table, where Nick was sitting with Frankie Concetti and Zach Mason, guys he'd known since he was a kid—and all firefighters, with the exception of Frankie, who only served on a volunteer basis. The rest of his time was devoted to the family restaurant—a fixture in town, and one that would definitely be passed down through the generations if Maria Concetti had any say in it.

"So Frankie," Jonah said once they all had cold beers in

front of them. "Have you found a nice girl to please Mamma Maria yet?"

Frankie shot him a look of warning. "She's getting worried. Thinks I'm an old man when I'm barely over thirty."

"Hey, I thought you were older than me," Jonah joked. "Unless you were a child genius who started school a few years early."

Frankie didn't look amused. "Mid-thirties, then. Or at least nearing them. To hear my mother say it, I may as well be in my mid-fifties! She keeps telling me that she could have had five grandkids by now if I'd been more serious about settling down."

"But you date all the time," Zach pointed out, failing to mention that he did too.

"And none of them are keepers." Frankie shook his head sadly while the rest of the guys laughed.

"Who's going to take over the business if you don't start a family?" Jonah asked, only half-seriously because he knew that Frankie was a romantic at heart, always on the quest for his better half.

"Now you sound like my mother." Frankie sipped his beer, the mood lightening as much as Jonah's spirits. "Besides, you should talk. And you—" He shot a glance at Zach who just gave a mild grin in return.

"I'm not in a rush," Zach replied. "You can't hurry these things."

"Not to hear my mother tell it." Frankie sighed deeply. "I'm her only child. She keeps threatening to give the restaurant to one of my cousins if I don't continue the bloodline soon."

"She wouldn't do that!" Jonah knew that Maria Concetti adored her son as much as the town loved her sauce, a recipe that Jonah had tried to replicate without success for years.

"No, but only because she doesn't think any of them can cook as well as I can. The other night I heard her bragging to one of her sisters about my meatballs!" Now even Frankie was laughing.

"What about your restaurant plans, Jonah?" Zach knew when to change the topic, and Frankie looked relieved to be off the hot seat for the night. "Nick told us you put an offer on the space next to the bakery."

Right next to the bakery. The words hung there, and he knew that all the guys were thinking the same thing as him. It was far from ideal, and not just because it prompted the Sunrise Sisters to consider an expansion. There wasn't anything alluring about working next door to Becca if she was hating on him.

Jonah took a sip of his beer. "Still waiting to see if it's accepted."

"Well, don't look now but the other bidder just walked in the room." Nick couldn't fight his grin.

Jonah's mouth went dry. Since when did Becca go out for drinks at this joint? But then—why shouldn't she? A sudden thought took hold, and he wrestled against the pounding of his heart when he stared back at Nick.

"Is she...seeing anyone?" He tried to keep his tone casual,

but he could hear the blood rushing in his ears over the din of the room.

Becca had always put that bakery over everything else, and he knew firsthand how tiring the days could be in the restaurant business. Becca had early days, working in the kitchen well before the sun rose, and long hours on her feet.

It was grueling, but not for those who loved it. It was a love in itself. Greater than all else. Even if it didn't leave time for much else.

"Why?" Frankie cut in. "You still love her?"

"No!" Jonah protested, pretending to find the thought ridiculous. Preposterous. But the truth was that of course he loved her. He'd never stopped. He thought of her every day he was away, wondering what she was doing, picturing her in the bakery, comforted by the image of her rolling out dough or greeting a customer with that bright smile.

He'd held onto that image, even dared to think that nothing would have changed, that when he came back, they might stand a fighting chance.

Now he was afraid to turn around. To see if she was with another guy.

"She's not dating anyone to the best of my knowledge," Nick said.

Jonah closed his eyes briefly, feeling the relief seep through him. If anyone knew the secrets of the Sunrise Sisters, it would be Nick, considering that he was dating one. Jonah took another sip of his beer and glanced over his shoulders to see Jill, Becca, Carly, and Joanna collecting glasses of wine from the bartender.

Nick's hand shot up again and Jonah braced himself,

knowing that the women were going to come over to the table. He was looking forward to the opportunity—but from the way Becca's face darkened when she glanced over at them, she didn't feel the same way.

And neither did Jill.

"Look at this," Nick said when the group arrived at the table. "One big happy family."

Far from it. And they weren't family, yet.

Frankie was clearly enjoying this new development. "My mother can't stop talking about it. Sharon Parker and Robert Quincy. The old man finally wore her down."

"More like she finally came to her senses," Jonah joked, hoping to keep the mood light.

He thought he saw a small smile flicker across Becca's mouth, but all too quickly it was gone.

"Let's pull over some more chairs," Nick started to say, and Carly happily nodded, until Becca flashed her a warning glance that was far from subtle.

"It's girls' night," Joanna cut in, sensing the tension. "And I suppose it's guys' night for you."

"One of these days your fiancé has to join us," Nick told her. "My dad said they're working the residents extra hard at the hospital."

"Then maybe as a doctor with a longstanding reputation there, your father can ask the administration to loosen the schedule. Then I might have time to finally plan my wedding."

"I'm sure Becca would love to help," Jonah said. "Did she mention we're planning our grandparents' wedding?"

"The *two* of you?" Joanna slid a glance at Becca. She clearly hadn't been told.

Beside him, Frankie snickered, then covered his hand with his mouth, his big shoulders shaking.

Becca pursed her mouth. "Yes, well, with the wedding in only two weeks, they need all the help they can get." She motioned to the bar. "We should probably order before all the tables fill up."

Jill cast Jonah one last look—a warning, perhaps, to let them be in peace—and linked arms with Becca as the women walked away, Carly trailing behind after giving Nick an affectionate look that lingered long enough for Frankie to whistle. Even Jonah had to laugh at that, relieved not to be on the receiving end.

Still, he marveled at how Nick's life had come full circle.

Nick had moved back to town with his young daughter after his marriage broke up; if anyone knew a thing or two about second chances with the Parker women, it was Nick.

Jonah leaned across the table. "Come on, Nick. You gonna help me out?"

Nick raised an eyebrow. "With Becca? Or is this about the Sunrise Sisters' desire to expand the bakery?"

Jonah wasn't foolish enough to enlist Nick's help in asking the Parker women to back down.

Sure enough, Nick said, "Carly's already making lists of how she plans to use the space. She even has Daisy pulling out her colored pencils and drawing up her vision."

"You're joking," Jonah said flatly, even though he had the sinking sensation that Nick wouldn't elaborate this much on a prank.

"Sorry, Jonah." Nick shrugged. "But those women are a force. If they have decided they want the space, it will take something major to make them back down."

"They may not have a choice," Jonah countered. "Denise is the one making the decision."

"Which is probably why I saw Becca knocking on her door on the way over here tonight." Nick took a casual sip of his drink.

"You didn't," Jonah said, straightening his shoulders, his mind already spinning through ways to get Denise's attention—and coming up blank.

Nick's grin widened. "I didn't. But I wouldn't be surprised if she did."

No, Jonah thought as he picked up his glass. He wouldn't either.

When Becca wanted something, she poured her entire heart into it. It was one of the things that had drawn him to her, and one of the things that had made him fall in love, over and over, the more he spent time with her. He never tired of seeing her eyes light up, or her smile, still radiant, even after a long day of work. She was passionate and committed.

And once, he'd been the one she committed to—for life.

He glanced over at her, catching her in a moment where she started laughing at something Joanna had said, her wide smile on full display.

She'd loved him once. And love didn't just end—he knew that all too well.

The question was, had she stopped?

SEVEN

With the bakery closed on Wednesdays, Becca saw that as an ideal time to devote to her grandmother's wedding plans. It was a quiet morning at Nana's house, something that Becca had gotten used to over the years, first after her mother had passed, and later, after the sisters had grown up, Jill moving into her own cottage, and Carly heading to Philadelphia for college where she'd ended up staying for ten years.

Nana, however, never got used to it, and she liked to say so too.

"Carly had Daisy over last night," Nana mused. "Nick was at the station and Carly decided to have a girls' night in, me included. We baked cookies and watched a princess movie. That little girl knew the words to every song and she wasn't shy about singing them, too. I'm thinking of asking her to be my flower girl unless you think that's too presumptuous?"

Becca didn't need time to think about it. Nick and Carly

may only be recently reunited, but their feelings for each other were hardly new. If anything, their relationship was only proof that some people were meant to be together, regardless of circumstances that may have kept them apart.

Some people, Becca reminded herself. But not all.

"I think that is a lovely idea. Daisy will be thrilled!"

Nana's smile sobered. "What about you? How do you feel about the wedding?"

Becca looked up from the wedding magazines they'd been flipping through and gave her grandmother her full attention. "I'm happy for you, Nana. I've been worried about you since you retired from the bakery. That business was your entire life."

Nana nodded. "It was easy to make it my whole life, especially after your grandfather died and then your mother followed. Work kept me busy. And the friendly faces kept me from feeling too alone. And of course, I had you girls there with me."

"I sense a but coming on," Becca said.

"That's just the thing, Becca," Nana said. "I didn't even realize that there should be a *but* until it was almost too late."

Becca reached out and squeezed her grandmother's hand. "But you did realize it. *Before* it was too late."

Nana nodded. "I think that when there's something missing in your personal life, it's easy to fill that space with distractions. Don't get me wrong. I loved working in the bakery. I miss it every day. But it didn't leave much room for anything else. Because I didn't allow it to."

Becca had the sudden impression that they were no longer talking about Nana's nuptials at all.

"I assume you've heard by now that we're thinking of expanding into the space next door," Becca said. "We planned to tell you Saturday night, but obviously there were other things to talk about that day."

"Robert told me. And I've been wanting to tell you girls that you have my full support. Growing the business is part of making it your own." Here, Nana paused.

"But?" Becca raised an eyebrow.

Nana looked at her expectantly. "You haven't told me how you feel about Jonah being back in town."

"And bidding on the same property?" Becca shrugged and turned a page in the magazine. "What's there to say? It's his hometown, too."

"Surely, it had to be a surprise, though," Nana remarked.

A surprise was an understatement. Gone were the days of her fantasizing that Jonah might roll into town, apologize, and give her back the ring that had graced her left hand for nearly a full year. By the time she'd accepted that was never going to happen, she'd hardened her heart, until she no longer wished for it. No longer felt disappointed that it didn't happen.

And now it had. When she'd truly given up. On the dream. And on the man.

Becca sighed and closed the magazine again. She'd already read through so many of these when she was engaged that she didn't really need any more ideas. "I haven't thought about Jonah in a long time, Nana. The bakery helped with that."

Nana sighed. "I'm sure it did. But I also know that you haven't made much time for romance. Since I've already established that you can't blame the long hours, then that makes me wonder if you might..."

Becca widened her eyes. "Still have feelings for Jonah?" She laughed, but not one of amusement. "I can assure you, Nana, that the only feelings I have for Jonah are negative."

Nana looked sad. "But you two used to be so close."

"That was a long time ago, before I saw how selfish the man can be." Becca tipped her head. "Jonah will always put his ambitions and passion over all else. And anyone else."

"Maybe so." But Nana didn't look convinced. "And here I thought that when you offered to help with the wedding, it might be a chance for you two to get close again."

"It will be a chance for me to make sure he doesn't screw things up for you," Becca corrected her grandmother. "I want this to be special. We all loved Mr. Quincy long before you realized that you did. Even if he is Jonah's grandfather," Becca added with a grumble.

"What's this about Jonah's grandfather?" came a voice from the hallway.

Becca turned around to see Mr. Quincy standing in the entranceway to the living room, Jonah not far behind him. He was carrying a large box, and he looked just as displeased to see Becca as she was to see him.

Nana shot Becca a look of apology but something in her gaze wasn't quite as contrite as it could have been. "I forgot to mention that Jonah and his grandfather were stopping by with some of his things so we can sort through all of our belongings and decide what to keep and what to part with before we officially combine our homes."

"Forgot?" Conveniently omitted was more like it.

Right. This was her cue to leave. Becca returned the magazines to the end table. "I should get going anyway. Jill and Carly will need me at the bakery." Even though they weren't open for business, Wednesday was often used as a day of prep, making the second half of the week a little easier.

"Oh, they'll be fine. Remember what I said about not letting that place become an excuse?" Nana whispered as she scooted by her to greet her next-door neighbor turned fiancé with a tender kiss.

Jonah met Becca's eyes over the elderly couple's heads and comically widened his eyes. She bit her laugh to cover her smile. She wouldn't bond with him over this.

"Jonah, it's so *nice* of you to give your grandfather a hand," Nana said when she and Robert finally pulled away from their rather lingering embrace, if Becca did say so herself.

"I had time. And there are just a few more boxes to bring over for the day," Jonah said.

"Have you decided what to do with the place when you move in here?" Becca asked Robert, both out of curiosity and any excuse not to look over at Jonah, much less speak to him.

"Oh, Jonah will be taking over the house!" Mr. Quincy beamed with pride at his only grandson, but Becca struggled to hide her shock.

He was going to live in the house next door to Nana's? While it made so much sense, she wasn't sure why she hadn't considered the possibility, it also didn't make any sense at all.

"That sure you'll be getting the space next to the bakery, are you?" she asked after Nana and Robert had disappeared into the kitchen under the excuse of making some tea but more likely so they could have a little privacy.

Or give Becca and Jonah some unwanted privacy, Becca thought.

She stood there, in her own childhood home, feeling downright uncomfortable by the presence of the very person who had visited hundreds of times over the years, until he was nearly as much a staple as her grandfather's old reading chair.

Now, Jonah seemed taller and appeared to take up more space in the front hallway, out of place amongst the framed family photos that lined the walls. The one from their engagement had long since been removed.

"It was always my intention to open a restaurant here in town," Jonah told her.

Once it had been his dream. His plan. All he'd ever wanted. Now it was reduced to an intention. Maybe that's all his proposal had been too, when she'd dared to think it was a promise.

"Yes, but we both know that there is only one storefront available on Main Street and my sisters and I have just as good a chance at getting it as you do." If not better. Everyone knew that the bakery was the heart of the town.

"I guess we'll see," was all Jonah said.

"I guess we will." Becca huffed out a breath and walked toward the door, but the front porch was blocked with boxes stacked waist-high. "A couple of boxes? This is more like fifteen!"

"You can get out of here faster if you give me a hand," Jonah said. He bent to pick up another box, catching her eye. Despite the tension that lived between them, there was a glimmer of something—understanding, if she didn't know better.

Becca felt her defenses drop, but only a little. "I wasn't trying to get away from you. I should get back to the bakery, that's all."

"Aren't you guys closed on Wednesdays? A few minutes won't make a difference," Jonah said, pulling a box from the top of one stack. "Besides, you're going to have to take some time away from the place to help with the wedding preparations."

"About that...I think it's probably best if we divide and conquer." Actually, maybe this impromptu meeting was for the best. It saved her from having to deal with him later.

Jonah set the box down with ease and looked at her squarely, his gaze trailing over her face until she shifted on her feet.

"What did you have in mind?"

"I made a list of everything that needs to be done," she said, pulling her phone from her pocket. More like she'd pulled open the folder she'd shoved deep in a desk drawer and tried to forget. Going through the magazine clippings had reminded her of all the ideas she'd had for her own wedding, and she was eager not to think about her own wishes, but instead focus on practical matters, taking Nana's tastes into consideration. "The invitations have been ordered and sent directly from the printer. The venues are locked in. That leaves the flowers, the music, the cake, which my sisters and I will be making, and the tuxes for the men."

"Wow, you're really on top of this," he remarked.

"Yes, well, I have experience with this already."

At that, his cheeks turned a little ruddy and he broke her stare. "Bec—"

She held up a hand. "We're here to talk about our grandparents, that's all. I can text you the list. Is your number still the same?"

He nodded. "Wasn't sure you still had it. You never used it."

She stared at him, her heart pounding with anger and hurt. "Yeah, well, I didn't think there was anything left to say." She pulled his name up in her contacts list, hardly believing that something that once felt so normal now seemed so strange, attached the list, and sent it. A moment later, she heard a ping.

"There, that was easy enough. Now, let's just hope the rest of the planning goes as smoothly."

"I'm sure it will," Jonah replied.

"Well, we tried to plan one other wedding together, and look how that ended up," Becca said as she sidestepped around the boxes and hurried down the front path to the sidewalk.

She didn't know what she had been thinking, offering to plan this event with Jonah.

But sometimes, it was best to keep your enemies close.

~

By Thursday morning, Becca was grateful to be busy again. Baking calmed her, and the customers gave her purpose. She watched as a little girl with blond curls and chubby cheeks took one of their newest items—a pink cake pop dipped in sprinkles—into her outstretched hand with eyes round with wonder and delight.

"This looks too pretty to eat!" she told Becca.

"But it's also too delicious not to eat," Becca confided.

The little girl giggled before trying a small nibble, then proceeded to eat the entire thing in three bites, before her mother had finished paying.

"I can tell that we'll be back soon," the woman said, tousling her daughter's hair fondly.

"Please do!" Becca replied, and gave the little girl a wave goodbye.

She sighed with contentment as she wiped down the front counter. It was days like this that Becca loved everything about her life here in Hope Hollow. The joy she brought to people, and the happiness they gave her in return. It was what got her through the days of doubt, when she wondered if Jonah had been right, that there was more than this bakery to life.

She was still smiling when the door jangled again and there, in the doorway, was Denise.

"Becca! You're just the person I wanted to speak to this morning." Denise bustled up to the counter with a big grin on her face.

Good news? Or a kind way of sugar-coating bad news?

Becca felt her heart swoop and then speed up and she

glanced toward the kitchen doors for one of her sisters, but they were nowhere to be seen.

This was it. A decision had been made. Once again the fate of this bakery was at stake.

"Yes?" she managed, her voice tight in her throat.

"I woke up with an absolute craving for those blueberry muffins you make," Denise said. "And I need to talk to you about your grandmother's wedding!"

Becca blinked at the woman, realizing that this was, indeed, the entire reason for her visit. She nodded and started to plate one of the best-looking muffins in the basket.

When she handed it over, she gave a sheepish smile. "Here I thought you might be coming to tell me you'd made a decision about the space."

"I'm sorry it's taking me so long," Denise told her. "But I just want to make sure that I make the right decision. That store was my baby, and even though the space will be used for a different purpose, I can't help but care about its fate. Is that silly?"

"Not at all," Becca told her. She remembered just how much it had weighed on her to think of what might happen to this bakery back when they thought they might have to sell it. Even though it would have a different name, new items, and new ownership, somehow it would always still feel like hers.

"It would have been so much easier to have a daughter or granddaughter to pass my business down to," Denise said a little sadly. Then, forcing a smile that didn't quite meet her eyes, she said, "Actually, I do have something to share with you, though." She retrieved a sketchbook from her tote bag.

"Nana's wedding dress?" Becca leaned in closer as the door chimed. She glanced up to see none other than Jonah strolling over to the counter.

She felt her temper flare as her pulse quickened, but in the company of Denise, she did her best to hide her true emotions.

"Well, isn't this convenient!" Denise exclaimed, smiling up at him.

He grinned broadly in return, his gaze resting on Becca in a way only she could detect was challenging.

Becca gave her sweetest smile, "Isn't it?" So very convenient indeed.

"I was just about to show Becca the design ideas I have for her grandmother's wedding dress," Denise said. She flipped through the book, stopping on a detailed sketch of a traditional shift dress with three-quarter-length sleeves. The skirt grazed the knee, and the neckline was adorned with crystals.

"Oh!" Becca gasped.

"You think she'll like it?" Denise asked eagerly. "I wanted your opinion before I ran it by her. Of course, I'm open to suggestions—"

"No suggestions needed," Becca said confidently. "You are an amazing designer and this sketch is proof of that."

"I always liked to get to know my brides individually so I could make sure they had a dress that fit their style."

Becca gave a little nod. "I remember," she said quietly. She and Denise had spent hours combined sharing ideas, analyzing sketches, and deciding on the best materials, and the right amount of sparkle.

Now Denise's cheeks flushed and she lowered her eyes, no doubt remembering those many meetings, too. Closing her sketchbook she said, "Oh, I'd better sit down or I'll end up spilling something on this drawing before your grandmother can see it. Now, how much do I owe you?"

"It's on the house," Becca told her.

She thought she heard Jonah give a little snort as Denise patted her hand and then carried the muffin and coffee to a table.

"On the house?" Jonah raised an eyebrow as he leaned into the counter. In the clear morning light, Becca could see the flecks of brown in his otherwise grey eyes framed by dark, long eyelashes that she once hoped a future daughter might inherit.

She quickly looked away.

"It's the least I can do for the woman who designed such a beautiful dress for my grandmother," Becca wiped some crumbs from the counter, avoiding his eyes.

She was grateful that Jonah wasn't drawing attention to the other part of the conversation, about the other dress that Denise had designed, that had never been worn—at least, not by Becca. The one Denise had insisted on returning the money for, even when Becca told her that she'd earned every cent of it. In the end, Becca had insisted Denise kept it—she hadn't paid for it and she'd never wear it.

Had Denise gone on to sell it to another bride? It had been years, so it was entirely likely. But Denise had been kind enough never to say and Becca couldn't bear to bring herself to ask.

"Besides," Becca said. "It's not like you're completely innocent."

"What's that supposed to mean?" Jonah asked, a defensive edge creeping into his tone.

"Oh, I just think it's interesting that no sooner than Denise walked in, you were all but ten steps behind."

Jonah gave her a look of exaggerated insult. "Becca. You can't be accusing me of stalking that sweet old woman."

"If she hears you calling her old, you can kiss that storefront goodbye." Becca pinched her lips to fight her smile and slid him a look. "Why else would you be here?"

He shrugged. "For the same reason as everyone else. To grab something decent for breakfast. You know I could never resist your chocolate chip scones."

"Well, it's too bad that we only have cinnamon today then," she said.

From the glimmer in his eyes, he didn't look very deterred. "Guess that means I'll have to come back again tomorrow."

Now she let out a sigh. "Jonah, why are you really in here? Is there something you need to say to me?"

He held her gaze for so long that she was starting to regret asking him that question. There was nothing to discuss, not when it came to her and Jonah.

"I went over your list for the wedding," he said. He licked his bottom lip. "It was very...thorough."

"Well, there's a lot of little details to consider when planning a wedding. Did you think about what you'd like to handle? The music, perhaps?" If he dared to say the cake, then she'd know he was only looking for trouble. She and her sisters had been brainstorming the design all morning while they baked.

"I talked to Frankie about the menu, and I can handle the music, but the truth is that you know your grandmother better than I do. And I know you want this to be special for her. For both of them."

Becca nodded along. That was true. But she wasn't sure she liked where this conversation was going.

"And?"

"And," he said. "We might have a better result if we...collaborate."

"Collaborate?" She barked out a laugh. "Yeah. No."

"But you didn't even think about it," he protested, following her down the side of the display case while she straightened baskets and trays.

"I don't need to think about it," Becca said. "I can handle most of this, Jonah."

"But wouldn't my input be nice? On behalf of my grandfather?" he countered.

She set her hands on her hips, exasperated, if only because he had her there. "Why is it okay for you to make quick decisions without consulting me but I am supposed to consider your feelings?"

"Whoa," he said, backing up. "Something tells me we aren't talking about wedding planning anymore."

"Oh, we are. Just not this one." Becca took a breath, suddenly all too aware that she was getting emotional, and she thought she was all out of tears for this man. She swallowed hard and looked up at him, hating the softness she saw in his eyes. "Please don't make this more difficult than it needs to be."

They stared at each other for a moment, no words spoken, but so much said in the silence.

Finally, Jonah leaned forward, whispering so softly that against her will, Becca had no choice but to lean in as well to hear him. "You do know that she's over there watching us, don't you?"

Becca gave a subtle glance over his shoulder to see Denise quickly look away and flip a page in her book when it was quite clear that she probably hadn't skimmed the first page.

"Something tells me that we have a lot to gain if we both play nice and get along," Jonah added, pulling back.

"I am playing nice," Becca said, affronted. "And for my grandmother's sake, I'm willing to get along."

"Is that the only reason?"

"Why?" Becca asked. "You think that I'm only doing it to garner Denise's approval, like you?"

Jonah's eyes went a little flat. "Here I thought it might be because you still enjoyed my company."

She frowned at him until she started to wonder if he meant it and—maybe worse—if that was his true intention.

But then she thought about the space next door. And Jonah's plans. And how Jonah's plans always served one purpose—himself.

"Fine. We can collaborate. But only because our grandparents deserve a nice wedding," she warned. Just saying those words sounded so...*weird*.

"Meet tonight to discuss?" Jonah asked.

"What did you have in mind?" Becca was wary.

Jonah shrugged. "Concetti's?" Perhaps sensing her hesitation, he added. "We both have to eat and maybe Maria will let us sample some of the food she plans to make for the reception."

Becca sighed, seeing no room to argue. It would be efficient.

And it most certainly would not be a date.

So why did it suddenly feel like one?

eight

This wasn't a date. This was Concetti's, the neighborhood Italian restaurant—and also the very place where Jonah had proposed, dropping to one knee while Maria Concetti wept into a hanky and called out her son Frankie to serve them with a complimentary bottle of champagne.

Before they had even left the restaurant, the phone lines had rung so many times that the only people who didn't know the happy news yet were the ones that had been deliberately spared: namely, Jonah's grandfather, and Jill and Nana.

Even the gossip mill knew that some things were sacred.

Once, this place had been. But now it was just Concetti's, the only place in town to grab a decent plate of fettuccine alfredo or a large cheesy slice, or of course Maria's tiramisu, which the Parkers all knew to be made better than they could ever do it—if they dared.

It wasn't a date, but it sure felt like one as Becca pulled open the door to the small establishment to be greeted by the sounds of European sidewalk cafe music softly playing over the speakers. In the evenings, Maria liked to light a candle on each table, anchored in an old wine bottle dripping with wax.

Maria hurried across the room when she saw Becca. "Becca! Is your grandmother joining you tonight? Oh, I heard the news! Isn't it wonderful! At long last! Robert Quincy only chased after her for the past decade, if not more! About time she gave the man a chance! I always told Sharon she could be too stubborn."

"I'm afraid it's a Parker family trait," Becca said, thinking of Jill, who was so much like their grandmother at times it was almost funny, except when it wasn't. But even Jill wouldn't turn away a man's dinner invitations for ten solid years.

"Well, your grandmother certainly took her time letting him in!" Maria continued.

"And that's why she's not wasting any more time. Are you sure you can pull everything together by next Saturday?"

"Please! I love cooking for a crowd." Maria brushed off her concern. "And it's not like Frankie's giving me any grand-kids to cook for."

Becca could only laugh. "I'm helping my grandmother with her plans, so if you need anything, don't be shy."

"Becca." The woman set a pudgy hand on her arm. "Have you ever known me to be shy?"

Becca laughed again, but it was interrupted by the flash of Maria's dark eyes.

"Oh, I can't believe this. Coming into my restaurant? No, no, no." Maria grabbed Becca by the shoulders and gave her a shove behind a tall faux fig plant. "You wait here. *I'll* take care of this."

Maria swung her dish towel over her shoulder and marched to the door just as Jonah was walking up the steps to the glass-paned door.

"It's okay, Maria," Becca insisted, even though her stomach was telling her otherwise. Just the sight of Jonah in dark jeans and a button-down shirt made her heart swoop. "I'm actually meeting him."

Maria's eyes flew open. "Him? The man who shattered your heart?"

"Well, I wouldn't say he shattered it..."

"The man who jilted you? Running off to California like that?" Accusation was hot on Maria's face. She glanced at the door and back to Becca. "You're a more forgiving woman than me, Becca."

Not really, Becca thought. "His grandfather is marrying my grandmother," she pointed out.

"Robert is cut from a different cloth," Maria said, her eyes narrowing as Jonah approached through the glass.

"Mamma Maria!" Jonah used the local nickname fondly as he opened the door.

Maria gave him a hard look. "That's Maria Concetti to you," she said, before turning and walking back toward the kitchen in a visible huff, no doubt to pick up the phone and make a call to Debbie at the flower shop across the street.

That reminded Becca that she should probably pay a visit there tomorrow and get a start on the centerpieces.

To Jonah, she couldn't help saying in a singsong tone, "Someone's in trouble."

Jonah frowned deeply. "And here I thought Maria and Frankie were happy to host the event."

"Oh, they are," Becca told him. "But not for you." She smiled sweetly.

"Then it's a good thing I'm not planning this thing on my own." Jonah looked a little bewildered as he stood in the entranceway of the restaurant. "I guess we can sit wherever we'd like?"

There were a few other couples already dining, but a table near the window was open, letting in the early evening light. It wasn't until they'd sat down that Becca realized this was the exact place they'd been sitting the night Jonah proposed.

"We can move if this table upsets you," Jonah said.

So he remembered, then.

And clearly, so did Maria. The woman halted as she approached the table, her eyes widening before she came over and dropped the breadbasket on the table.

"Wine?" she asked, looking only at Becca.

"What's a meal without it?" Jonah said pleasantly.

To that, Maria gave a little harrumph and turned on her heels to walk over to another table.

"I'm more than fine sitting here, Jonah. What happened between us is old news." Becca picked up the menu, even though she already knew what she would order. It was easier than looking at the man across from her.

"Not to everyone," Jonah said, glancing at Maria. "I guess she's never forgiven me for what happened between us."

"Yes, well, people in Hope Hollow can be protective of

each other," Becca replied. She hoped that Maria did bring the wine and soon. She could use a little something to take the edge off right now. It wasn't easy, sitting here, directly across from the only man she ever loved, with nowhere to look but at his still handsome face or a menu that hadn't changed since she'd been born.

"What about you?" he asked, setting his menu on the table, looking her in the eye until she was forced to return his gaze. "Have you forgiven me?"

She stared at him sharply, and then, seeing the hurt in his eyes, felt her shoulders relax. As easy as it would be to blame him for their breakup, she could have followed him to California instead of staying put.

"We both made our choices." And they hadn't chosen each other.

"Yes, but I was the one who threw a wrench in our plans." His forehead creased. "I'm sorry, Becca. For...all of it. At first, I was sorry that you didn't want to come with me. Now, well, now I'm sorry I ever went."

This wasn't what she was expecting to hear any more than she'd ever thought he'd want to move back to this small town after leaving it for more exciting pastures.

"Why?" she asked. "Because the job didn't work out?"

"That, sure, and because of what I lost. We were good together, Becca."

She steeled herself against the softness in his eyes, his kind smile, and all the memories that accompanied it. Good times out on the lake in the summer, or even here, at this table, after a long day on their feet. He understood her back then, the way she loved what she did as much as it exhausted her, that she took pride in her effort, and that she aimed to please.

Once, he'd said that he admired her dedication to the bakery. Until he made her choose between it and him.

"We were good together," she agreed. "But not good enough in the end."

He sighed heavily, nodding his consent. "Maybe not."

She sensed some hesitation as his brow furrowed and the silence stretched between them, but she wasn't going to continue this conversation. Not here, at the table where they'd gotten engaged, where the diamond solitaire first graced her finger and sparkled in the candlelight. Not where they'd excitedly talked about their life together—all that was yet to come.

Not now. Maybe not ever. Not when none of those plans and hopes had ever happened.

"You look...really nice," Jonah said quietly.

Despite herself, Becca felt her cheeks warm. She didn't need her ex-fiancé thinking that she'd gotten dressed up for him—not when she'd made the effort for herself. To feel good in her own skin. Confident in her position in life.

Maria returned then with a bottle of red wine that she set on the table with two glasses. "Ready to order?" she asked Becca pleasantly.

"I'll have the spaghetti Bolognese," she told the woman with a smile.

"I'll do the same," Jonah said, clearly hoping to keep things easy. But Maria just gave another harrumph in return and, grabbing their menus, walked away.

Becca laughed as Jonah poured the wine. "Sorry, but you have to admit it's a little funny."

"Not really. If more people feel like she does, then I'll have a pretty empty restaurant come opening night."

She didn't point out that she had just as good of a chance of getting Denise's space as he did. No, she was more curious about his intentions, long-term. Once, opening a restaurant here in town had been all he talked about. And then one day, he just gave up on that dream.

"You're really planning on doing that then."

Jonah filled his glass and set the wine bottle back on the table. "I wouldn't have made an offer on the dress shop if I wasn't."

"But why the change in plans?" Becca had to know.

"The job in California didn't work out." Jonah's shoulders looked heavy. "And this was just the excuse I needed to give my notice."

Becca nodded. So that was it then. It took another career opportunity to bring him back to town. Nothing more than that.

"Should we toast?" Jonah asked, lifting his glass.

"To our grandparents," she said, finding it to be the only safe topic right now.

And the only thing still binding them together.

Jonah knew better than to extend the meal into dessert, and not only because Maria Concetti had been giving him the stink eye for the last hour. When the bill arrived, placed squarely in front of him with a hard look, he was more than happy to pick up the tab.

But not for the night to be over.

"I can walk you to your car if you'd like," he offered when they stepped outside into the cooling evening air. It was still light outside, but dusk was quickly approaching.

Alone with Becca like this, it felt strange to be walking a few feet apart, when the last time he'd lived in town, he would have reached for her hand, or slid an arm around her waist.

He slanted a glance at her. Her nut-brown hair still hung at her shoulders, her nose was still slightly upturned, and her lips always slightly parted in a smile. Even her sundress was one he'd seen her wear a dozen times at least—one he could still remember the feel of under his fingertips.

So little had changed. But too much had.

"I walked to work today since it wasn't my day to run the deliveries," Becca replied. "Besides, I want to stop by my grandmother's house and share some of our ideas with her."

Over the meal, they'd exclusively talked about the wedding, even though it was clear that Becca was leading the conversation. He was fine with listening to the voice he'd missed so much, happy to have an excuse to stare at her lovely face, which seemed to have only grown more beautiful in the past two years.

"You're heading my way then," he said.

"It's okay. I don't need a lift," she was quick to reply. "I like to walk, especially after a big meal."

"I know. I happened to walk into town too."

He saw a shadow of frustration pass over her features but

then, for lack of an excuse to protest, she shrugged. "Okay, then."

They walked down Main Street until they reached the very end, and then turned once they reached the small park, where they used to sit on a bench, holding hands, enjoying the peace and quiet, and the sounds of each other's voices. Back then, they had so much to talk about, but, like now, they were equally comfortable saying nothing at all.

At least, it used to be comfortable. Now the silence that stretched between them felt heavy and empty, like a space that needed to be filled, a distance that needed to be gapped.

Their grandparents' houses weren't far, and Nana Parker's house was lit up, filled with life.

"Carly lives here now," Becca said, finally breaking the silence only once they were just outside the driveway. "She moved back a few months ago."

"So I'm not the only one who has recently returned to town?" Jonah tried to make the conversation light, but Becca's face remained serious.

"I don't see her car, though." She seemed disappointed by this. "She's probably out with Nick."

"I was surprised to learn that they were back together," Jonah confessed.

Becca gave a little smile. "When Carly came back to town, it was clear that there was still something between the two of them."

"Meant to be," Jonah agreed, nodding.

"More like...unfinished business." Becca held his gaze for a moment and then looked away. "I should go in before it gets too late." She stared at him as if waiting for him to go.

Jonah remained where he was. "I'm still a gentleman. I haven't changed all my ways. I'll watch you go in and then I'll leave. Promise."

Becca shook her head, mumbling goodbye before turning away. As promised, he watched as she walked up the path to the house and opened the front door—but before he could walk two yards toward his grandfather's house, she was hurrying right back down the path again. Sprinting, really.

"What's going on?" He stood firmly in his spot, his heart starting to race. Becca's expression was wide in horror until he realized as she drew closer, that she was also laughing.

"It was my grandmother. And—and—" She laughed so hard she doubled at the waist. "My eyes! The image is burned into them!"

"Oh, no." Jonah looked over to his grandfather's house, which was dark and empty looking.

"They weren't..."

She sputtered on a laugh as she nodded. "Oh, they were."

Jonah tried not to picture what she must have seen. He'd known his grandfather as a loner for so long, a sweet old man, mostly content with the company of a dog. "Let me walk you back to town then," he said.

"But I told my grandmother I'd stop by tonight to discuss the wedding plans," she said, still catching her breath.

He raised an eyebrow. "You really intend to interrupt them just now?"

Becca grimaced. "They didn't see me. I suppose I can try back in...a bit."

Jonah saw an opportunity and quickly said, "I don't suppose you'd want to come in then. You can wash your eyes and maybe we can have dessert, given that I was probably at risk of having a tiramisu thrown in my face if I'd tried to extend the meal at Concetti's."

Becca laughed again, and this time something in his chest warmed because she wasn't laughing at what she'd just witnessed at her grandmother's house. She was laughing with him. Like old times.

"Come on then. Unless you want to go back in there?" Jonah gestured toward the house next door, not wanting to think of what must be going on behind those walls.

But happy for another excuse to spend more time with Becca.

Becca hadn't been in Mr. Quincy's house since Jonah had left town, and now she was very aware of what was missing from it. The dog bed sat empty, but the food and water bowls had been tucked away. A red collar and lead still hung from a hook near the door.

"Your poor grandfather. He must miss his dog so much," she said, her heart heavy at the image of the old Lab that had kept the man company for so many years.

"He's had a lot of heartache in his life." When Jonah's parents died in a car crash when he was twelve, Jonah became the man's only living family.

And vice versa.

"I miss that dog," Jonah said, frowning deeply. "I wish I'd been able to say goodbye."

Becca saw the flex of his jaw and felt her guard come

down. A part of her wanted to reach out, rest a hand on Jonah's arm, and comfort him in some way. But it was no longer her role to do that, and this was a painful reminder of that.

She could still want the best for him, but she wasn't the one to give it.

"Your return is good timing all the same," Becca said gently. "I know how sad Mr. Quincy was these past few weeks. You being here has to brighten his spirit."

"Along with your grandmother." Jonah looked out the window that faced Nana's house and turned to give her an exaggerated grimace.

She couldn't help laughing again. She was surprised to find how easy it was to enjoy his company, once she let herself.

"So, what are you making for dessert?" she asked. Food was the one thing they still had in common that was a safe space—no emotion, no history, just a shared interest.

He gave her an arched look. "What am *I* making? You're the pastry chef."

"Baker," she corrected.

"Please," he scoffed, pulling two aprons from a kitchen drawer and handing her one. "You can bake circles around the pastry chef at the restaurant I came from."

"The one in LA?" She was surprised to hear this, and she knew he wasn't just flattering her, either. This time she couldn't fight off a smile. "But I thought it was one of the best restaurants on the West Coast. I thought it was—"

The opportunity of a lifetime.

"Things aren't always what they appear, are they?" Jonah asked.

Becca wondered if he was only talking about the restaurant, but she knew that he wasn't. It was a true statement, and one they'd both understood, from a young age. When she'd lost her mother not long after Jonah lost both his parents, they were bonded by the loss, a shared experience that they wouldn't have wished on each other—on anyone. At school and around town, they had to go about their business, and it was easier not to talk about it, not to let the emotions creep in and bury them in the past. But when they were alone, walking home from school, they shared their innermost feelings.

Jonah put on a brave face. Even when inside, he felt something different.

Now she wondered if he still did that. If maybe, he was doing it now.

"So what am I making then?" she asked. She'd be happy for the task, anything to keep her from looking into those deep-set eyes.

"What are *we* making?" he clarified. He narrowed his gaze mysteriously and walked over to the fridge, pulling out ingredients until she'd figured it out without him even telling her.

"Peach cobbler?" The fruit was the giveaway, of course, along with the canister of brown sugar he reached for on the counter.

"Can't beat a classic," he said, rinsing the fruit.

Becca moved to get a cutting board; she knew her way around this kitchen nearly as well as Nana's. Back when they were first dating, in their late teens, they alternated between the two houses, usually based on who had the best ingredients to work with on any given day. Sometimes they experimented with new recipes gleaned from a cooking show or a magazine, but often they fell back on family favorites they wanted to share with each other.

Peach cobbler had been Jonah's mother's favorite. And his too.

"Oh! That's Carly's car." Becca saw the headlights through the window over the sink. A moment later she heard the door open and close and Carly was walking up the path to the front door. "It's too late to warn her."

Jonah looked as amused as Becca felt as he came to stand next to her, staring out the window, waiting for Carly to dash back out, scandalized.

They watched and waited, and Becca was all too aware of the way her hip was pressed next to his, how she could feel the rise and fall of his body, the warmth from his skin. Her breathing felt heavy, and she stopped thinking about her sister or grandmother at all until Jonah gave her a little nudge.

"Well, she didn't come out screaming," Jonah observed.

"I guess it's probably safe to go back to my grandmother's now." For some reason, Becca wasn't as relieved as she should have been. She took in the ingredients that were spread on the countertops. The fruit hadn't been cut yet, and it didn't make sense to stay now, especially when there wasn't a handy excuse.

Besides, did she even want to stay?

She saw the resignation on his face when he nodded.

They'd been saved, just in time. Before they fell back on old ways. Before they lost sight of where they now stood.

"This time, I'll probably ring the doorbell." She offered a smile because not doing so suddenly felt wrong.

Coming back here tonight had stirred up good memories. Reminded her of all the things she liked about Jonah. About the two of them together.

Maybe, somehow, there could be a way to hold onto that part of the past. Even if the future didn't include him.

"You might want to get into the habit of that going forward," Jonah agreed. "Maybe we can meet again. To plan the wedding," he added quickly.

She hesitated, but then nodded when she saw the question in his eyes. "Maybe just not at Concetti's next time."

He grinned more easily. "Maybe I'll give you a call then?"

"You have my number," she said.

He always had, she reminded herself. He'd just chosen not to use it.

And that was something she needed to remember in order to guard her heart—the one that he had broken.

nine

Carly beat Jill and Becca to work the next morning, and Becca wasn't entirely surprised. When she'd stopped by Nana's last night, Carly was already in her room, and Nana looked more than a little flushed.

Her younger sister was rolling out a pie crust when Becca finished tying her apron strings and started on the muffin batter.

"I didn't see you last night when I stopped by the house," Becca said casually.

"Oh...." Carly's cheeks turned pink. "Nana had Mr. Quincy—I mean, Robert—over and I was tired so I just... went to my room."

And shut the door and turned the lock, no doubt.

Becca nodded. "Last night made me start thinking that it might be best to knock before I stop over at Nana's again."

Carly's head shot up. "And best for me to move out!" Her eyes were so wide that Becca started to laugh.

"Something tells me I missed something," Jill remarked. "And that I'm probably glad that I did."

"Oh, very glad," Becca confirmed. She looked back at Carly. "Are you really serious about moving out of the house?"

"Living there was only supposed to be temporary while I got settled in town."

"Are you and Nick thinking..." Jill let her thought go unfinished, but Becca was wondering the same. Were Carly and Nick already taking their relationship to the next level?

"Are there going to be two weddings in this family this summer?" Becca was both surprised and pleased. Love had finally found the Parker women—or at least, half of them.

Carly's cheeks turned even pinker, but there was no denying the joy in her smile, despite how hard she tried to fight it. "We're not there yet. But in the meantime, I do think I need to find something temporary. Nana and Mr. Quincy deserve some privacy."

"Why don't you move in with us?" Jill suggested. It was a small cottage but the third bedroom, while tight, could probably fit a bed and dresser. Right now it was mostly used for storage.

"Really?" Carly's eyes lit up. "Okay. But it won't be permanent. Just—"

"Temporary," Jill finished. "Meaning until Nick pops the question."

Becca couldn't help but feel a twinge of sadness, remembering the weeks leading up to her own engagement. She'd been dating Jonah for ten years by then and had known him even longer than that. It wasn't a surprise, per se, but it had been exciting all the same. Her future had been planned out for her since she was a child standing on a stool to be able to work at this very counter. She'd always known she would take over Sunrise one day, along with her sisters, but knowing that she and Jonah were going to share a life together just completed that picture.

"Enough about me," Carly said. "Have you heard any more from Denise? I have to admit that I've been dreaming about how long our pastry case could be if we had double the space. Think of all the new recipes we could fill it with!"

Carly's enthusiasm was contagious, and soon they were all tossing out ideas for new flavors they might try, or stations they could have, perhaps multiple cases for cakes and cupcakes, one just for cookies, and another for savories.

Becca stopped herself before she got too carried away with this fantasy. "Denise is busy working on Nana's dress, but she said she plans to have an answer by the wedding when her work is done."

"Has Jonah said any more?" Jill asked. Then, sensing Becca's hesitation, she added, "Come on. There's no denying that you've been spending time with him."

"Only because we both agreed to help plan the wedding!" Becca was aware that both of her sisters were staring at her, and that neither seemed to be buying her excuse. "That's all it is. There's nothing else between us."

"If you say so," Carly said, her tone implying that she didn't believe it.

"I do," Becca said. Because someone had to be sensible here, even if it was becoming increasingly difficult to be just that.

When the bakery closed, Jill offered to prep for the next day and Carly helped with the cleanup and offered to run the leftovers over to the fire station where Nick was on shift.

Becca was on her way to the flower shop when her phone beeped. Thinking it could be her grandmother or one of her sisters needing something, she stopped to check it. Her heart sped up when she saw Jonah's name on the screen.

It had once been such a regular thing. Now, it felt strange. And maybe, a little good. Maybe, too good.

Dinner tonight?

She stared at the text, knowing that he had said he'd contact her but still surprised that he actually had.

That he'd kept his word.

Before she could reply, another text came through: I can pick you up at 7. Thought it might be more productive to try something in the next town over.

In other words, he wasn't willing to face Maria Concetti again. And there weren't many other options for dinner in Hope Hollow unless you wanted pub grub at the local watering hole or an expensive meal at one of the inns.

She looked up to see Debbie's nose all but pressed to the window of the door at the flower shop, then quickly tapped out her reply: Ok.

It was just a one-word reply, but why did it feel so big?

Almost as big as the other one-word response she'd given when Jonah had once asked a much bigger question.

Becca's heart was hammering when she shoved the phone back into her bag and walked into the shop where

Debbie pretended to suddenly be interested in spritzing some flowers with water, realizing all too late that she hadn't been inside since—

"Becca Parker!" Debbie feigned surprise and greeted her with a warm hug. "Why, I haven't seen you in my store in *years*! Not since—" She stopped herself, realizing that she'd gone too far.

"It has been a long time," Becca agreed. But somehow, right now, it felt like no time had passed at all. Having Jonah back in town was bringing up all sorts of memories— the good and the not-so-good. Much like this cute little shop that she had avoided since she'd last been in, picking out flowers, struggling to decide between the endless options.

"Well, it's a good thing that I get a craving for the bakery's oatmeal cookies at least twice a week then!" Debbie gave her a wink. "Tell me, to what do I owe this honor?" Suddenly, she gasped, then brought a hand to her mouth. "Is your wedding back on?"

Becca was now the one to gasp, then give a little laugh to cover her reaction. "Um, *no*."

"Oh." And cue the look of pity. "I'm sorry, hon. It's just that with him back in town I thought that maybe you guys might have decided to reconcile."

"We broke up two years ago," Becca pointed out. As if anyone in Hope Hollow needed to be reminded.

"True, but when it's meant to be, love finds a way. Look at your sister and Nick!"

There was no sense in comparing her relationship with Jonah to Carly's breakup and reconciliation with Nick. Nick and Carly had been torn apart by circumstances—Jonah had left by choice.

And she'd chosen not to follow him.

There was always that reminder, tucked away, an irrefutable fact that made it impossible to place all the blame squarely on him, even though it was often tempting.

"I'm actually here for my grandmother's wedding," Becca clarified, getting right down to business and quickly off the topic of her personal life. "I'm sure you've heard that she's getting remarried."

"Who hasn't?" Debbie remarked. "Now that was quite a shock! Not that we're all not happy for her, but she's been on her own for so long that we just assumed it would always stay that way. That she wasn't open to love."

Becca frowned at that thought for a moment. Debbie wasn't far off base. For a long time, Nana had been closed off from opening her heart again. A broken heart could do that to you. Becca knew all too well.

"I'm helping her with some of the plans and I thought I might see what's in season," Becca said.

"Of course! I received my invitation this morning, and I must say that Sharon certainly didn't leave much time for me to put in orders with my contacts, but I'm sure that I can come up with something perfect for her. Let me get my portfolio. I can show you what I've done for some other weddings—" Again, Debbie stopped herself, putting a hand to her forehead when she reached the counter. "But then, you've already seen the book."

"It's been a while. And I'm sure you've added to it since then."

"Of course!" Debbie looked relieved. "Styles are always changing and I have to keep up with the trends!"

Becca took the large, leather-bound binder from the woman and tried not to remember how it felt in her hands the first time she'd held it. How exciting it had been to come into this shop, not for a gift or a holiday arrangement, but for her wedding. How she'd struggled to narrow down the color theme, eventually settling on a colorful palette, inspired by the cakes she liked to decorate.

She steadied herself as she flipped to the back of the book, wanting to see the more recent photos.

Debbie lingered on the other side of the counter, tying a ribbon around a vase of long-stem roses. It was clear from the way Becca kept catching her glances that she had something on her mind.

"I heard that you and Jonah had dinner together last night."

And there it was.

Becca knew better than to be surprised that Debbie should know. She was likely first on Maria's speed dial, and from there the phone chain began.

"We're helping to plan our grandparents' wedding," Becca replied, not looking up from the book. "Maria has offered to host the reception."

"Was that all it was then? Business?"

Becca thought about that for a moment. Maybe, that's all it ever had been between them. Then and now.

"Sorry, hon. I was just hoping that maybe there was a little more to it. That he came back into town, hoping to make amends, win back the heart of the only girl he ever loved." Debbie sighed. "What can I say? I'm a romantic. Being surrounded by beautiful flowers all day will do it to you."

Becca gave a wry smile. "I'm afraid the romance is better left to your customers then. I can report that there is nothing going on between me and Jonah."

Only she wasn't so sure of that, not any more than she could be sure that she was the only girl he'd ever loved. Once, she had been. But he'd been away for two years. Surely in all that time, he would have met new people. Maybe even someone special.

"I guess I was holding out hope that he came searching for a second chance," Debbie said with a shrug. "It happens. My Rick and I broke up once. Now, we were only eighteen and it was only for two weeks, and I can't even remember what the argument was about, seeing as it was too many decades ago to count. But second chances do happen."

They did, for some. But the way Becca saw it, she'd already used up her second chance in life—they'd managed to save the bakery, and it was a reminder of just how important it was to her and her sisters.

She looked back at the book, flipping quickly past the photos that had inspired her own choices, the arrangements and centerpieces that has never been made.

Jonah had come back to Hope Hollow for a second chance, all right. But not for a future that included her.

If anything, it was one that could once again impact her bakery. And the people she loved most.

Jill's cottage looked the same as it had years back before Becca had moved in. Cheerful and sweet, quite unlike Jill Parker, who hadn't so much as cracked a smile at him since he'd been back in town, even though they were about to become family. Jonah was relieved when Becca emerged from the blue front door the moment his car pulled to a stop outside so he was spared having to knock.

His gaze raked over the yellow sundress she wore, the way her brown hair bounced at her shoulders when she took the stairs quickly and hurried to the car.

He didn't put it all together until she fastened her seatbelt, slightly out of breath.

"Jill doesn't approve of us having dinner together two nights in a row?" he guessed. Another person who wasn't ready to forgive him yet, it would seem.

Becca looked a little ashamed. "It's book club tonight. She assumes I'm there."

"Oh, well, we can do this another night." The truth was that the wedding plans were just an excuse to meet up; she'd handled most of it already and all he had to worry about were the tuxes and music for the reception, which they'd agreed last night would be a playlist.

"It's okay," Becca said, surprising him. "I didn't even read the book."

His heart sped up a little that she hadn't jumped at the chance to make a quick getaway. Maybe, she wasn't regretting agreeing to this night.

"You never did," Jonah said with a fond smile as he drove the car toward the end of the block. She'd been in that book club for as long as he could remember, and he'd often sent her with some appetizers for the other women who seemed to enjoy the wine and the food more than literature, not that he was complaining. Becca always reported back what the women said about his dishes, and he'd always taken note.

"I always intend to! I just...never find the time."

"Or make time?" Jonah countered. "I get it. Life gets busy. The days slip away. And before you know it—" Before you know it, years have gone by. Choices have been cemented. And it was too late to undo them.

"So you didn't make time for a book club in California then?" she joked. She knew the only things he read were cookbooks and autobiographies of celebrity chefs.

"That would be a no." He followed the road out of town, the sense of being alone with Becca more obvious by the moment. The radio was on, but too low to hear, and she still wore the same perfume that would linger in the car long after she'd stepped out, leaving it to smell like vanilla and flowers. Leaving him to think of her. "I didn't make time for much of anything. The only people I ever met were on staff. And they were just as miserable as I was."

"Then why stay so long?" she asked.

It was the very question he'd asked himself, a hundred times, if not more. Certainly, more since he'd been back here, in this town.

"I guess I felt like I had to try to make it work. I sacrificed so much to go there, it didn't seem right to give it up so quickly."

She fell silent beside him and he wanted to say something more, something closer to the truth. That he was afraid of what would happen if he did come back. If he'd tried to get her back—and failed. Instead, he'd accepted his own choices, and hers. Made the best of it. Until he couldn't anymore.

"Is history going to repeat itself?" she asked.

They'd reached an intersection and he stared at her, trying to understand what she was asking.

"If you don't get the space on Main Street," she elaborated. "Are you going to stick it out here or admit defeat?"

"I don't like to admit defeat," he said with a grin. And in this case, he didn't intend to.

Not with the restaurant. Not with finding a way to make her change her mind.

About the space. And about him.

The town of Mapleton was close, but unlike Hope Hollow, it had a bigger commercial district, one that had grown even more in his short time away.

There were plenty of restaurants to choose from, and while he usually cared about where he ate, appreciating good food, and wanting to sample other chefs' creations, tonight wasn't about a culinary experience.

Tonight was about spending time with Becca. While he still could.

They agreed on the Italian restaurant, hoping that word wouldn't travel back to Maria or anyone who had her phone number, and found a parking spot a few blocks away. The evening was warm with a cool breeze, and the sun wouldn't set for a while.

It was a perfect summer night, like so many they'd spent

together before. Ones he'd taken for granted. Ones he'd walked away from.

"Isn't that—" Becca stopped walking, but Jonah didn't need to follow her gaze to know what she was talking about. It was the diner up ahead on the corner with the booths lining the window where people sat, enjoying hamburgers and fries and laughing like they didn't have a care in the world.

But Jonah couldn't laugh. Not anymore. Not when he knew what the place used to be.

"My parents' restaurant." He nodded. They'd wanted something in Hope Hollow, always kept their eye on the properties page in the Sunday newspaper, and always kept an ear out for anyone who might want to give up a coveted storefront on Main Street.

It never happened. Until now. And Jonah had one chance to make his parents' dream come true. To fulfill the wish they'd made for themselves.

"Do you want to go in?" Becca asked tentatively.

Jonah stared at the restaurant, so different than it was when his parents owned it. He'd never been inside since it traded hands not long after their deaths. Couldn't even bear to look at it, really. Once it had been a bistro, its windows lined with curtains his mother had made, that matched the ones in the small apartment they'd lived in upstairs when he was just a baby, before they'd scrimped and saved for the little house in Hope Hollow, closer to his grandfather.

He must have passed his childhood home a hundred times, if not more, always filled with nostalgia, always a little sad when he saw the front door open and another woman emerged to water her flowers.

But the restaurant was different. This was where he remembered his parents the most. His dad in the kitchen, teaching him proper knife skills at an early age, his parents experimenting with the menu that they kept fresh, writing the specials on a big easel that they'd prop up in front of the door, right on the corner for all to see. Back then, there had been candles on the tables, in little glass jars. Jazz music every Friday and Saturday night. His mother kept note of every-one's birthdays, and he used to follow his parents out along with the small waitstaff when they sang to the guest of honor, a candle flickering on a fat slice of his mother's chocolate cake.

It was a happy place. More a home than his actual house because this was where his parents came alive, doing what they loved, making him a part of it—from helping in the kitchen to naming their peach cobbler special after him. And it was the place that had inspired him to become a chef. Back then, he'd thought he'd eventually work for his parents, alongside them, growing the family business and taking it into the next generation.

But plans changed. They always did, didn't they?

"There's no point in going in," Jonah said gruffly. "The place is unrecognizable now." Every memory of his parents had been wiped out, replaced with red vinyl booths, bright lighting, and, from what he could see through the windows, kitschy uniforms.

"I'm sorry, Jonah. I know how much you miss your parents." Becca's eyes were soft with understanding.

He didn't need to say anything, he knew, because he didn't have to, not with Bec. With a tight nod, he shook himself from his self-pity. "I'm not the only one to know a loss."

Like him, she had no choice but to keep moving forward. But unlike him, she'd clung to those she had left.

"But I have the bakery," she said now. "Being there, in the kitchen, it keeps my mother with me. So does Hope Hollow."

"And that's why you'll never leave." He nodded. He knew. She'd told him that, clearly, but even before she'd said it, he'd known when he'd told her about California that she wouldn't go with him.

But he'd gone anyway.

"I thought it would be easier to get away," he admitted to her now.

She looked at him in surprise. "To forget instead of hold on?"

"I wasn't exactly doing my parents proud waiting around for something to become available in Hope Hollow and working in kitchens of random restaurants in surrounding towns. My parents had bigger dreams. I thought I found one of my own. One that they'd approve of. One that might... finish what they started."

"But what they started was right here."

"They always wanted a restaurant in Hope Hollow. In their own community. And they never got a chance to make it happen." Jonah gritted his teeth against the sadness that still caused him, the loss of not just their lives but a dream that had never come true. "They worked so hard, every day, and I just thought—"

"You thought that if you opened a restaurant on Main Street you'd be finally giving them the one thing they were never able to have." Becca's expression proved that she understood.

He nodded. And he was close, so close, but now, looking at the old bistro turned diner, he had the horrible sense that it wouldn't change anything. It wouldn't bring them back.

And it would only ensure that he and Becca were over. For good.

ten

Becca was in the bakery on Monday, still trying not to think about her last conversation with Jonah and instead about the fact that they were running very low on chocolate chip muffins and she could only hope that Carly was pulling another batch out of the oven when Erika walked up to the counter.

"Good morning!" Becca greeted her.

"I was afraid you wouldn't be very happy to see me," Erika confided in a low voice.

"If you're worried about me, you don't have to be," Becca said. "I can handle Jonah."

"How's that going?" Erika asked in nearly a whisper.

Becca was about to ask which part, but then she assumed that Erika, like everyone else, was probably more curious about the personal nature of her relationship with Jonah. And surely if Denise had some news on the space next door, she wouldn't have been shy in saying so.

"As well as can be expected," Becca said honestly.

She doubted that anyone had caught wind of their dinner in Mapleton, which had centered solely around the wedding plans, but she could tell by the less-than-subtle spark in Erika's gaze that their dinner at Concetti was just short of front-page news.

"You may have heard that my grandmother is marrying Jonah's grandfather." No sense pretending that it wasn't happening. And this weekend, too.

Erika had clearly heard. Widening her eyes, she said, "And how's *that* going?"

"It's going," Becca said with a laugh. "Actually, we cemented a lot of the plans over the weekend. My grandmother loves the idea of having the reception at Concetti's. Maria's been such a good friend and supporter of our business, and of course, the food is delicious."

She'd braved another trip to the flower shop, too, this time with Nana, to decide on the centerpieces and the bouquets. That only left the cake, which she and her sisters had brainstormed more this morning while they baked, and the music for the reception.

And of course, the wedding dress.

Knowing that Erika hadn't just come into the bakery to chat about Nana's love life—or hers—Becca said, "What can I get you today? I'm afraid I just sold the last chocolate chip muffin, but we do have some fresh scones."

"Just a cup of coffee," Erika said. "I'm still trying to lose the baby weight from my son."

"How old is he now?" Becca asked, picturing the cherub-cheeked little boy who liked to put his sticky fingers all over the glass display case.

"Two," Erika said flatly, then both women burst out laughing. She looked longingly at the display case. "Oh, what's one more day? Those scones do look amazing."

"Trust me, they're worth every calorie," Becca said with a grin.

Erika seemed to hesitate while Becca poured the coffee into a paper cup and bagged the scone. She knew that Erika was always on the go and, unlike many of the other patrons, never stopped and took a seat unless she had her kids with her, who tended to leave more crumbs on the table than they consumed.

"I have to say that I'm happy to hear that you're taking the news well. Or, as well as can be expected," Erika remarked.

Becca set the bakery bag on the counter and frowned at her. "I'm sorry?"

Now, Erika's cheeks flushed. "Oh, you don't know? But I assumed you did! I thought that's what you meant when you said everything was going as well as expected."

"And I thought you were asking how Jonah and I were getting along," Becca said, feeling her chest heave with panic.

So Erika did have news after all. And given that Becca had not heard directly from Denise, she had to wonder if Erika had been sent as the messenger. To deliver the bad news.

She glanced to the kitchen door, wishing one of her sisters was here for moral support. Now that some news might be presented, she honestly wasn't sure what she was ready to hear it. Getting the space had felt like a pipe dream, but when she thought of how excited she and her sisters, especially Carly, were about making the bakery more of their own, she knew they'd be very let down if they didn't get it.

And that Becca would be stuck with Jonah next door, day after day.

She closed her eyes, feeling the blood rush in her ears.

"It isn't easy to say this," Erika said with a heavy sigh. "There's been another offer on the space next door."

"Oh." Relief flooded quickly, slowing Becca's heartbeat, and making her smile wider than she had all morning. If no decision had been made then there was still hope. "Oh, well, that's…"

"Not good," Erika said firmly.

Becca's smile slipped again. Her hands squeezed the paper coffee cup.

"Is it a good offer?" she forced herself to ask.

"Higher than both of yours, but that's all I can say. And I probably shouldn't have said that much." Erika's eyes flicked over the bakery.

"So you can't tell me who it is?" Becca knew she was calling in a favor, but she was curious. She knew what she was up against with Jonah, but a mystery bidder left her on poor footing. Would this person be buttering up to Denise, dropping by her cottage with gifts?

"It's not anyone you know," was all Erika said, and her expression confirmed that she had said all she could.

That meant no one from town, then. Maybe, that would work to their advantage, considering how important the community was to Denise.

"Well, I appreciate the warning," Becca said, even though

there didn't seem to be much to feel grateful for at the moment.

"You might want to consider raising your offer," Erika suggested.

Becca felt her shoulders slump. "We already made the highest offer we could afford. And Denise implied that it wasn't just about money to her."

"No," Erika conceded. "It's not. But sometimes, it can tip the scales, make a decision a little easier."

Becca nodded, knowing that was probably true. "Thanks for the warning. I've been trying not to get my hopes up, but I'm not sure the same can be said for Carly."

Or Jonah, she thought, feeling a little sick. She knew what the space meant to him—or had, back when she'd thought his dream would last a lifetime. It meant carrying on his parents' legacy, doing what they couldn't. Cooking their recipes the way she baked her mother's. Having an outlet for the pain of loss.

A way to keep them alive, in some form.

"Well, if you do decide to raise your offer, let me know. You know I'm rooting for you," Erika said with a wink.

Becca watched her go and then stared wearily at the display case. All this time she'd been wondering what would happen if they got the space next door—and what would happen if Jonah did instead.

Now that there was the possibility that neither of them would get it, she suddenly felt like they were on the same team again, going after a shared goal, not separately, but together.

They'd come too far and lost too much to have someone else come over and sweep the plans out from both of them.

One of them was going to benefit from this.

And right now, she wasn't sure who she wanted to have it more.

Jonah was at the park when Becca left the bakery after another long, successful day. She'd waited four hours to send him a text after Erika left, only to see if he'd reach out first, but her conscience was getting the better of her, and she knew that she wouldn't feel right not sharing what she knew.

He probably assumed that they were meeting for more wedding plans. But she couldn't exactly tell him her real reasons, not until they were face to face.

It had been almost three days since she'd seen him, and she was surprised by the nerves that danced in her stomach as she approached him, looking relaxed and handsome, the way he was on so many occasions when a meeting like this was part of her daily routine.

"You called. I came." He grinned, and Becca had to push back the swell of attraction that was still there. Maybe it always would be. And maybe it would always be just that. A longing for something she'd once had, but an acceptance that it was long gone.

"Can we sit?" She motioned to the bench, dreading what she was about to say. Her sisters had been disappointed when she'd told them the news, especially Carly, who just as quickly brightened and said that it was just another offer, and who knew for what purpose. There was no way that Denise was going to hand over the keys to her boutique to something like a laundromat or tobacco store.

Now, as she sat, Becca almost felt like her sister's hope was contagious, until she remembered the financial end of things, and how indecisive Denise was being.

She sighed deeply.

"Long day?" Jonah asked, sharing the bench with her, so close that their legs were touching, even though there was plenty of space for them to spread out.

Becca considered inching over a bit, but there was something comforting about the proximity, about the bond they once shared.

About the problem that now united them once again.

"Erika stopped by the bakery this morning," she said. Seeing the question in his eyes, she decided to cut right to the point. "There's been another offer on the wedding dress shop."

"Another offer?" Jonah looked as stunned as she'd felt when Erika delivered the blow. "Did she say who made it?"

"Your guess is as good as mine." Here, Becca hesitated. She didn't know Jonah's financial position, but she assumed it was better than her own. When his parents had passed, they'd set up a trust, the very one that he'd planned to use to fund his restaurant years ago, while he was also saving up money and gaining experience at various restaurants in the area. It only made sense that he'd put the investment to the same use now.

But then she thought about what he'd said the other night. And what he'd said all those years ago. About how much that place would mean to him. How it meant putting his parents' deaths to new life, a new use. How it meant creating a legacy.

When she already had one.

And even though she'd lost her own mother, she'd always had something that Jonah didn't. Sisters. And a built-in home in that bakery. A place that was always theirs. A place that was part of their history, that carried the memories of generations that came before, and maybe even generations to come.

"She only said that it was a strong offer. She implied that I should consider raising ours," Becca added. Catching his eye, she said, "We aren't in a position to do that."

Jonah nodded. "Well, Denise did say that she wasn't basing her decision just on the money."

Still, Becca's heart felt heavy. "I guess I just didn't see this coming."

"I'm not raising my offer," Jonah announced.

She looked at him in surprise. "But if you can—"

He shook his head. "I'm not playing this game. We owe it to each other to do this honestly."

She stared at him, feeling her throat tighten at the gesture.

"It's getting late," Jonah said, changing the topic. "Maybe we can grab a bite to eat?" Sensing her hesitation, he quickly added, "We still have to confirm the playlist."

"I can't tonight," she said, happy for a legitimate excuse. She'd come here to warn Jonah, to be fair, just like he was proposing they do. It was nothing more than that.

It couldn't be, not with the choices they'd made two years ago. Not with the decisions they were facing now.

It was time to walk away, not fall back into their old ways.

Certainly not to fall back into love.

"No problem." He nodded, trying to show it was all right when she had a distinct feeling that it wasn't.

"It's my grandmother," Becca felt the need to explain, even though she knew she shouldn't. She owed the man nothing, after all. Or she shouldn't. "My sisters and I are meeting at her house to pick out our bridesmaid dresses."

Now Jonah lifted an eyebrow. "Will Denise be there?"

Becca felt her heart harden again, all those feelings of tenderness and connection gone with a simple question, bringing her back to their current circumstances. Reminding her of Jonah's priorities.

"She will. But we're all going to have a fitting. So don't think about finding an excuse to stop by, if that's what you're after."

He raised an eyebrow, giving her a playful look. "You forget that I've already seen you undressed."

Becca felt her cheeks color. "Yes, well, we don't have that kind of relationship anymore."

But she didn't know what kind of relationship they had. They weren't friends. They weren't family, even if their grandparents were getting married this weekend. They were just...two people after the same thing. And it wasn't each other.

The glimmer didn't leave his eye and Becca tossed her

hands in the air and started to walk away. "I mean it," she called back. "If that doorbell rings, I won't answer it!"

He caught up to her, slightly out of breath. "I promise I won't do that. But you have to admit that being with Denise tonight does give you an advantage."

Maybe. Or maybe not. Especially in light of the new turn of events.

"Denise is a fair person," she replied. "She's a person of her word."

But was Jonah? Once she'd thought so, but now, she couldn't be so sure.

DELIA ELISS

eleven

If it hadn't been for the dress fitting, Becca might have been inclined to spend the evening the way Jonah suggested. Instead, she told herself that she'd been spared—more time with Jonah just meant further heartache, didn't it? There was no other outcome in this situation, at least not from her vantage point. That dream they'd once had was long gone, replaced by separate ambitions. Ones that, for the second time, only served to drive a wedge between them.

When Becca arrived at the house in Jonah's car, she could only hope that her sisters hadn't spotted her through the windows. But when she let herself into the front hall, she saw that the rest of the women were already knee-deep in tulle and the front living room was transformed with a three-way mirror and racks of dresses in different lengths and fabrics.

She'd thought the beautiful clothing would be a distraction, but Jill looked at her sharply. "Did I just see you getting out of Jonah's car?"

Busted. Becca brushed a hand through the air, trying to show things were casual. And they were.

"He does live next door," she pointed out.

"I'm aware of that," Jill said, giving her a strange look. "It's not what led you both here that is so curious, it's more how you happened to be together in the first place."

"We are helping to plan the wedding," Becca said, walking over to the closest rack of dresses, her hand going to the peach ones that she had been considering for her own wedding party.

She quickly dropped her hand and turned, seeing Jill's eyes on her. Nana darted her gaze too, clearly interested but pretending not to be.

"If that's all it is," Jill said.

"Of course that's all it is." Becca felt prickly. "What more could it be?"

Jill said nothing and Nana's eyes were wide with interest, but Becca was the one whose spirits sank. She'd asked the question she hadn't considered herself—or had, but never voiced.

And now it had been answered. With silence. With nothing. With what she already knew.

There was nothing going on between her and Jonah other than a shared goal. And one that would be gone again in a matter of days, separating them once more.

"Where's Carly?" she asked, eager for a distraction.

"We're in the dining room!" came her younger sister's voice from the room across the front hallway. The French doors, which were usually open, were now closed, and after a bit of whispering and a little giggling, the doors slowly parted.

"Look at my flower girl dress!" Nick's daughter, Daisy, called, burst into the living room wearing a tea-length dress that flared at the waist, in the same fabric as Nana's wedding gown, only with a thick pink satin sash.

"Are those little pink roses along the neckline of your dress, Daisy?" Becca stooped for a better look, marveling over the details. She turned to Denise, who followed Carly into the room, looking nearly as joyous as Daisy. "When you said you'd be busy until the wedding, you weren't exaggerating!"

"Oh, these dresses are leftovers from my shop since I wouldn't have time to make anything custom other than Sharon's dress. But I can tailor them to fit. They're all just so lovely, it's so nice to see them have a home." Denise smiled wistfully at a pale blue chiffon gown as she adjusted it on the rack.

"I rather like that shade of blue," Nana said, coming over to take a closer look. "What do you think, girls?"

Jill, who had been sitting quietly in Grandpa's old armchair all this time, gave a nod. "I like it. And it's different than pink or peach."

Becca glanced at her sister, wondering if Jill was trying to spare her feelings. Knowing that she was.

"And it can be your something blue!" Daisy volunteered, still flouncing around in her dress.

"Let me see if I can pull together three options." Denise started rifling through the rack, pulling out dresses and handing them to Carly. After a few moments of contemplation, there were five dresses, all similar in color but different in style and material.

"These were all samples," Denise explained. "I don't have two of any of the same, I'm afraid."

"That's okay," Carly said cheerfully. "We're all a little different anyway."

Becca considered how true that was. Carly was the optimist of the group, always finding the bright spot even on the darkest days. Jill was pragmatic, sometimes too realistic, to hear Carly tell it. And that left Becca, in the middle, in every possible way.

But the one thing they all had in common was the bakery. And that was a good reminder for Becca to keep her head where her heart was: with her sisters, building their business, doing what she loved.

"But you girls are still so close," Nana pointed out. "They don't just call you the Sunrise Sisters because of the bakery."

"No, they call us that because we're usually up before sunrise," Jill bantered. "Not that it bothers me."

"Or me," Becca said.

"It never did. The smiles on your faces are what earned you the name," Nana said proudly.

"Hard work is good for the soul," Denise agreed with a sigh that was a cross somewhere between contentment and —if Becca didn't know better—loss.

∽

Jonah let himself into the back door of the house to see his grandfather eating dinner off a tray from the comfort of his easy chair, the television in the living room on a commercial break.

"It's a good thing Sharon Parker can't see this," Jonah said, walking into the room.

His grandfather wasn't concerned. "She knows that I enjoy some company with my meals, even if it is the sound of the television."

"I was referring to the microwaved dinner." Jonah knew that, like him, Becca's grandmother appreciated not just preparing good food, but taking the time to properly enjoy it, too.

"My days of eating like this are numbered, I'm afraid." His grandfather sighed and looked down at his tray. "But that's a good thing."

"For more than one reason," Jonah said walking back into the adjacent kitchen. He opened the fridge and called, "Let me at least make you an omelet!"

"I'm fine with this baked chicken," his grandfather said with a huff.

"There's nothing baked about it," Jonah pointed out. They both knew it had been nuked in the microwave.

Jonah began cracking eggs into a bowl, enough for them both. Eventually, his grandfather came to join him.

"Glad to see you came to your senses," Jonah said.

"I never said I didn't love a good meal." The old man smiled fondly. "But I don't know where you and your parents got it from. Certainly wasn't me."

"Grandma was a good cook." Jonah remembered the

woman as lively and happy, content with a quiet home life, and, like her husband, the companionship of a loving dog.

"As I said," his grandfather said. "It wasn't from me. Helen and your mother used to cook for hours in this kitchen. It wasn't a surprise that my daughter married someone who loved food as much as she did. It helps, having a common bond like that."

Jonah nodded. It did. Or it could. But sometimes, that kind of passion became a problem, driving two people apart rather than bringing them together. It was different for his parents, who shared a restaurant, building a dream. Even if it hadn't completely come true.

"You're thinking about Becca, aren't you?"

Jonah whisked the eggs. "No. Why'd you think that?"

"Because when I was fetching my dinner from the microwave, I looked out the window and saw her getting out of your car."

"So I gave her a ride. She was going over to her grandmother's for their dress fitting."

"I know." There was a gleam in Jonah's grandfather's eyes. "Seems to be going pretty well between the two of you. I wasn't so sure when she showed up for our engagement announcement, but since then—"

"Since then we've been busy planning your wedding. Not ours," Jonah reminded his grandfather.

"You know I kept your grandmother's ring," the old man said, trying to act casual when he took some sharp cheddar from the fridge. For a man who didn't cook, he certainly knew what he liked to eat.

"Well, it would have been strange to give it to Sharon

Parker." Jonah met his grandfather's eye, knowing this wasn't what the man was saying to him.

He could still remember when his grandfather had given him the ring, as if he could sense that the time was coming, that Jonah was thinking of proposing—and he was. He'd put it off for too long as it was, always waiting to be more settled, to have his plans for his own restaurant underway first, instead of working in other chefs' kitchens. His grandfather handing him that box was just the nudge he'd needed.

Maybe, his grandfather still had a way of quietly guiding him in the right direction.

Or maybe, he was getting caught up in Nana Parker's matchmaking schemes.

"Speaking of the past," Jonah said. "I'm in charge of music for the reception. Did you want to jot down some of your favorite songs?"

"I suppose it was too short of notice for a live band," his grandfather said with a nod of the head. For a moment he was quiet while Jonah melted butter in a pan and then added the eggs, bringing the heat down to a low setting. "I remember watching your parents dance in their bistro. They had that great jazz band that came every weekend and brought in the same people week after week. Your mother called it family night, because you always joined in, too."

Jonah's smile felt as tight as his chest. "I remember." The sound of his mother's laughter, his father twirling her near the bar. It wasn't just one of the best things about the restaurant, it was one of the best parts of his childhood.

Now, glancing at his grandfather, he realized just how much it had meant to him, too.

"Do you happen to remember the name of the band?" he asked.

To his disappointment, his grandfather shook his head.

Jonah sprinkled some cheese over the eggs but right now, his mind wasn't focused on the food. His grandfather may not remember the name of the band that used to play at his parents' bistro, but there was one person who might.

The doorbell rang just after Nana had returned her wedding dress to the garment bag. With some minor tailoring, it would be a perfect fit by Saturday, and even Becca was starting to feel excited as all the details came together. This was going to be their first family wedding—not her own, and certainly not as any of them could have imagined it, but special all the same. Maybe more, Becca thought, every time she saw the light in her grandmother's eyes.

"I'll get it," Becca said, already standing, but her pace stopped when caught Jonah's image through the windows that framed the door.

She pulled the knob with more force than necessary but she blocked his entrance by standing in the center of the doorframe.

"You have got to be kidding me," she said by way of greeting.

"I swear I'm not here to try to charm Denise." Jonah held up his palms in a show of innocence.

Becca folded her arms across her chest and gave him a

long look. His eyes were wide, earnest, and if she didn't know better, she'd say he looked a little...desperate.

She softened her stance. "Against my better judgment, I believe you. But what is your reason, then?"

"I need you," he said, silencing her.

It had been so long since he'd needed her for anything, not to taste one of his creations, brainstorm a recipe, or just give him a hug after a long hard day. Or long before that, when they were two wounded kids, quiet companionship.

But hearing him say the words, she realized how much she craved them. And maybe, how much she still needed him, too, even she'd put a firm stop to that the day his Jeep drove over the town line.

"I have an idea for the wedding, but I need your help."

So it was just about the wedding planning, then. All at once, the lightness that had come into her chest pulled down again, a weight reminding her of where they stood, and what they'd lost, a long time ago.

"Now?" The timing was inconvenient at best, and suspicious at worst.

"The wedding is only days away, so it's now or never. It might not even work out, but...I have to try."

I have to try. That was another thing he'd said to her when he told her about the job in California. He had to try.

She glanced over her shoulder, a quick glimpse into the living room, knowing that her presence was no longer needed. Her bridesmaid dress had been selected, tried on, and deemed to fit perfectly. Denise made most of her inventory in standard dress sizes, which kept things easy.

"Give me a minute," she said, going to close the door, but instead of leaving him on the porch as she'd planned, her grandmother came around the corner, beaming at the sight of him.

"Why, Jonah! You're just the person I was hoping to see!" She beckoned him inside with her hands. "Would you be a dear and help Denise carry all these dresses out to her car?"

"I'd be more than happy to do it," he said, grinning.

Becca narrowed her eyes at him as he scooted past her and into the living room.

Catching Jill's eye, she saw her sister's mouth pinch.

Jonah gallantly helped Denise with the garments, leaving behind the bridesmaid dresses and Daisy's flower girl dress. He carried the gowns carefully to the car, grabbing a fistful by the hangers in each hand and then returning for more.

One thing Becca had to give him was his speed. If he were looking to drag out an opportunity to kiss up to Denise, then he could have easily done it.

When he came back from the last trip, leaving only Nana's wedding dress in the protection of Denise's arms, he gave each of the women a smile and said, "If you'll excuse us, Becca and I have some important wedding business."

For a moment, Becca's heart lurched. Once, there had been a time when they had important wedding business. When they'd talked about food and music and venues and even cake flavors. Sure, Becca was the one placing orders, but Jonah was always happy to listen to her big ideas or offer some suggestions of his own.

Carly gave Becca a less-than-subtle glance when she

hurried out the door, following Jonah as he cut across the grass to his grandfather's driveway, where his car was parked.

He opened the door for her, letting her slide onto the familiar seat. She eyed the glove compartment, wondering if she opened it, she'd find the same stack of old CDs he used to keep in there.

She kept her hands in her lap instead. She didn't know what would be worse, really. Seeing that everything was the same as it had been the last time she'd been in this car, or that the CDs they used to listen to were gone along with all the other things they'd once shared.

"So, what is this important wedding business?" she asked.

"The music," he said, tossing an arm around her seat-back as he reversed out of the driveway.

"And we have to drive for that?" She watched Nana's house pass by through the window, knowing that Denise and her sisters were still inside, and likely all talking about her and Jonah.

"It's not a long trip. Just the next town over."

The drive was short, and Jonah focused on the road while Becca fiddled with the radio knob, trying to find a decent station, a song that didn't feel suggestive or bring her back to another time, stirring up emotions that were best forgotten.

She didn't properly look up until he came to a stop, and then she turned to him, catching his frown, the intensity of his stare at the diner that had once been his parents' bistro.

"I thought...I thought you didn't want to go in," she managed to say.

His jaw was tense as he continued to stare through the windows of the restaurant on the corner. Then, with a click of his seat belt, he said, "As I said. Wedding business."

She hopped out of the car, meeting him at the front of the door, wondering if he was really going to pull the door handle because he didn't make any effort to reach for it.

"Do you want me to go in?" She knew this couldn't be easy for him, and maybe that's why he'd asked her to come along. To run an errand. For the wedding. But he still hadn't told her what it was that he was looking for in here of all places.

"It's okay." He pulled in a breath and grasped the brass door handle, probably the only thing that hadn't been changed since the change in ownership. "This is something I need to do."

Inside, the place was just as kitschy as she'd expected. A long counter replaced where she imagined the bar might have been, the wood now Formica, with red leather swivel stools where something sturdier and more comfortable probably sat. In place of what Jonah had once described as small tables covered with thick white tablecloths and candles were booths, each one anchored with a napkin container and a mini-jukebox.

Jonah slid into the nearest booth to the door. It would make for a quick exit, Becca thought. In silence, they picked up the menus that were already on the table and read them.

"I don't think we're going to find any signature cocktails here," she said, scanning the menu, imagining how Jonah must be inwardly cringing at the options, which were a step above ballgame fare and mostly catered to kids or teenage couples.

"When in Rome." Jonah gave a grim smile and glanced up at a waiter wearing a fifties' style costume. "Two chocolate shakes. Extra whipped cream. And can you tell me who the owner of this fine place is?"

The kid jotted the order on his notepad and jutted a thumb over his shoulder. "The woman at the counter."

Jonah nodded but didn't say anything more.

Becca stared at him after the waiter moved on to another table. "So, are you going to tell me what this is really about? Because I'm starting to think that you didn't bring me here just to approve some playlist unless you needed the jukebox songs for inspiration."

That pulled a wan smile from him. "Actually, that's not a half-bad idea. But no, that's not why I'm here. My grandfather said something to me tonight about the band that used to play here."

"The jazz band." Becca remembered him talking about it. He always seemed to perk up at that memory.

"He didn't remember the name and neither did I, but I thought the owner here might, from when she took over the place."

"Do you think they'd be available on such short notice?" Becca wasn't so sure.

He shrugged. "It's worth a try."

Becca nodded. She supposed that it was. That most things were.

"My parents always used to tell me that I had to fight for what I wanted most." Jonah's eyes went flat as he looked out the window, and even though he was sitting here, in what was once their old restaurant, she knew he was back in the original setup. The brass fixtures. The dim lighting. The velvet curtains.

Once, she might have thought that she was what Jonah wanted most. And it still hurt to know that she would always come second to something else.

And that maybe, she could be accused of the same thing.

The waiter returned and set down two large, chocolate shakes, complete with a cherry on top.

"Should we toast?" Jonah asked before she could take a sip.

She hesitated, not only because the shake did look good, but because she wasn't so sure that she wanted to hear what he would say.

"May the best man—"

"Or woman!" Becca raised an eyebrow.

"May the best person win." Jonah gave her a sheepish smile and took a long sip of his milkshake. "I mean that, Becca. No hard feelings this time around. We both love what we do, and that's worth fighting for."

More than each other? It was a question not worth asking because they'd already answered it. Two years ago. And again, now.

She poked at her whipped cream with the straw. "A few months ago, we thought we might lose the bakery."

He looked at her in surprise. "But that bakery has been a part of Hope Hollow for generations!"

"Yes, well, when my grandmother retired, some people stopped coming in. Turns out that they weren't just coming in for her treats, they were coming in for her company." Becca sighed, thinking back on those tough days. "Jill and I were on our own, barely keeping up, and there were some days when I wasn't even sure I loved it anymore." She glanced at him. "There were some days where I wondered if I made a mistake."

The words hung there, long unspoken, many times thought. She'd chosen the bakery over him, no different than him choosing that restaurant over her.

The space between his brow pinched. "You did the right thing staying here, Becca. You stuck with what you loved. Who you loved."

She swallowed hard because that was only partially true. She'd loved him. And she'd let him go.

"We had an offer from a corporate chain to buy us out," Becca continued. "But then Carly came back to town and everything turned around."

"How so?" Jonah of course knew that once, Carly didn't have any interest in working at the bakery.

"She had new ideas for improvements. And change. Changes that were scary at first, ones that felt like a risk. But they also felt exciting too." Becca leaned into the table. "It felt like my sisters and I were building something of our own. Taking the business into the next generation. Putting our stamp on it for the first time instead of just following the chosen path."

"You never just followed the chosen path," Jonah argued.

She raised an eyebrow. "Didn't I, though? When you asked me to come to California with you, a part of me wanted to go."

He blinked at her in surprise. "You never told me that."

"How could I when I didn't even feel like I had a choice? You were making me choose, but the decision had already been made for me, for as long as I can remember. Every Parker works at Sunrise. I always knew it. And the thought of giving it up, walking away..." She shook her head. "My family needed me."

"I needed you too," he said quietly. His gaze locked with hers, his eyes were dark and drawn at the corners, pulling at the space in her heart that she'd managed to ignore these past two years. Reminding her that it was still there. That maybe, it always would be. "But I knew. I knew as soon as I asked you that you wouldn't come. But I had to ask. I had to try."

"I'm sorry," she said, and it felt good to come out with it. She could blame him all she wanted—and she did, for initiating it all, for giving up on his dream and asking her to do the same—but she played a part in their breakup too. She'd seen the hurt in his eyes when she'd told him she wouldn't leave Hope Hollow.

It was the same hurt she felt when he'd made a choice that didn't include her.

"You have nothing to apologize for," Jonah insisted. "I was the one who changed the plans. I was the one who left."

"And I was the one who let you go." She shook her head, knowing there was no use in imagining how different things might have been if she'd gone with him. Would they still be back here, now? Would she have returned to the bakery while he opened his restaurant next door, without her standing in his way?

It might have worked out perfectly.

But she couldn't have known.

"No, Bec," Jonah insisted. "I was the one who put an end to what we had. And I regretted that. I still do."

Becca stared into his eyes, seeing the pain that matched her own, knowing that time had dulled the ache, just like it had created new memories in place of the ones they'd shared, new experiences that the other didn't know about.

"Thanks for coming here tonight," Jonah said. "It's...it's not easy."

She slid a hand across the table and squeezed his arm. His skin was warm against hers, soft, and achingly familiar.

"I know it's not. And I know that it doesn't look anything like the way you remember it."

"No," he said with an unamused laugh. "It doesn't. But somehow...it still feels familiar. Maybe it's the windows. Or the view."

She nodded and set her hand back in her lap, fighting the part of her that still ached for contact with him. "You learned to love food in these four walls."

"It was so much more than that, though." Jonah took in the space. "I learned what I love. That it isn't always easy, and some days, it's downright work. But in the end, it's worth it."

Worth it. That was something she'd considered too many times over the years. And once again, she had to ask herself the same question.

"So," she finally said. "What are your plans now?"

His eyes lit up the way they used to when they'd talk about the years ahead, the life they'd have, the recipes they'd make, and she saw that maybe he hadn't changed so much.

And that maybe, unlike her, he hadn't stopped dreaming all those dreams.

He started describing the plans for his restaurant, from the color of the walls to the warmth of the wood tones, the recipes he was experimenting with, the ones that worked, and the ones that needed to be tweaked. She listened, smiling even as her heart began to ache, watching as he came alive before her, showing that same excitement that had made her fall in love with him all those years ago.

It was a wonderful plan. And a beautiful dream. And she knew that the light in his eyes would be gone if it didn't happen. If he wasn't chosen for the space. If it went to her and her sisters instead.

For a moment she opened her mouth, to tell him he could have it, the dream he'd clung to all these years, when she'd shut them out, closed them away in a place where she couldn't be reminded of them, and how they had never come true.

But then she thought of her sisters, of how even Jill had grown excited about the possibility. How it would launch the bakery into the next generation, really secure their futures. At least professionally.

But personally? She knew where her life stood if the bakery stayed as it was. But she also knew that without a restaurant in town, Jonah had no reason to stay.

"Do you want me to come with you to talk to the owner?" she asked when they'd finished their shakes.

He thought about it for a moment and then shook his head. "It's probably something I should do myself, but…"

"I can wait here at the table," she offered.

"I guess after tonight I won't have any more excuses to ask you to dinner." Jonah looked at her until her heart began to thump against her rib cage.

It was true. The wedding plans had come together and Saturday was quickly approaching. And then, there would be nothing left but Denise's decision.

And the memory of these past two weeks.

"It hasn't been all bad, has it?" His expression turned hopeful. "Spending time together like this?"

She gave a small smile. "No," she admitted. "It's been...nice."

And that was just the problem.

twelve

The bakery rarely closed, especially on a Saturday, but today was special. Special enough to keep the front room dark and the sign turned, special enough to still bring the sisters to the kitchen before daybreak.

Becca looked at the sketch of Nana's wedding cake that Jill had finished the night before, knowing it would be a challenge—but not one they hadn't faced before. Wedding cakes always came with a bit of stress—not only because of their size and decorations but because they would always be remembered, photographed even. In other words: there was no room for error.

Jill whipped buttercream while eyeing the round cakes that were cooling on the racks. Carly and Becca had already piped and stored dozens of buttercream flowers just waiting to be transferred onto each finished layer.

"How much time do we have?" Carly asked for the third time, not that Becca minded because she'd forgotten too. There was so much to keep track of: picking up the flowers, getting ready, getting Nana ready, taking photos in Nana's garden, and of course, getting to the church, that it seemed almost impossible to do all of this and finish this cake.

"Frankie will be here in two hours," Jill said, sounding only slightly impatient as she patted the cakes, gauging their temperature.

They'd been here for hours already, mostly working in silence, but now there was no more waiting. The wedding day was here, and even though it all still felt a little surreal, the cake was proof that it was happening.

"Okay, let the building begin!" Jill blew out a nervous breath, mirroring Becca's own energy. They'd made many wedding cakes here at the bakery, of course, but never one as important as this. Nana wasn't just their grandmother; she was an expert baker who had taught them everything that they knew.

This was their chance to impress her. To thank her.

To absolutely not let her down.

"I've heard that most brides are so busy at their weddings that they barely even remember to eat their cake," Carly said after they'd assembled the first layer, complete with a curd filling.

"I can't imagine anything stopping Nana from enjoying a slice of wedding cake, especially when it's lemon, her favorite flavor." It was Becca's too.

"And her favorite recipe," Jill pointed out. She let out a shaky breath as she stacked the second layer and tapped the dowels into place for support. Even though Jill was the most devoted to following the recipes passed down through the family, they weren't as well received by customers when they were no longer made by Nana.

Becca knew, however, that in a blind taste test, she wouldn't be able to tell her grandmother's lemon cake from the one made by her sister.

"The only thing that matters to Nana is that we made it," Becca assured Jill.

Once the cake was fully assembled, the real work would begin, all the little details that would take it from a cake to a work of art.

They'd opted for a pale yellow buttercream instead of fondant—it was more traditional, and there was no denying that Nana liked her recipes best, even if she was impressed by the new treats they'd started selling at the bakery.

With the entire cake carefully frosted and trimmed with some tasteful piping in white, they began artfully arranging their buttercream flowers.

Like so many other times when Becca was engaged in a task she loved, she didn't even notice the time until she placed the final flower on the top tier and looked up to see that over an hour had passed.

"I think we're done!" Jill announced, stepping back to admire the end result.

Becca let out a little sigh and squeezed Jill's hand. "I can't believe we just made a wedding cake for someone in our family."

"For our grandmother of all people!" Carly gave them each a pointed look. "If she can find love then there is abso-lutely no excuse for either of you. Especially you, Becca."

"What are you implying?" Becca asked. Not too long ago, her sister was hoping she'd join the dating pool.

"Jonah's been pretty helpful with the wedding," Carly remarked.

"Carly," Becca groaned. She waited for Jill to remind Carly of all of Jonah's wrongdoings, but her older sister was too invested in turning the cake and looking for any last imperfections.

"Learn from Nana," Carly said. "She turned down poor Mr. Quincy's advances for years and they lost all that time together. When she finally gave in, she fell in love. I don't think I can ever remember her being so happy."

"Jonah is hardly his grandfather, and I am hardly Nana," Becca replied.

"I'm just saying, don't hold on to things for too long. Nana wasn't ready to move on from the past. Look what happened when she finally did." Carly untied her apron strings.

"You're saying that I should get back together with Jonah?"

Carly turned from the hook where she was now hanging her apron. "What's so wrong with second chances? Worked out for me."

She gave a cheeky grin and picked up her overpriced handbag—the only reminder that she had spent far too long in a big city, thinking she was chasing a new life when she was really just running away from the one she had here. Most days, Becca felt like Carly had never left.

Maybe that was all it was with Jonah, too. It was easy to

pretend that years of not seeing each other had never happened.

"Well, I'm off. I have to pick up Daisy before heading back to the house. I'll see you both there?" Carly was already pushing out the screen door.

"Shoot," Jill said, looking at the clock in alarm. "I was supposed to pick up our bouquets twenty minutes ago! That was the one thing I was in charge of for the entire wedding."

"Other than this cake!" Becca reminded her. "I'll clean up here and wait for Frankie. See you at the house soon?"

Jill nodded, grabbed her handbag, and walked out the back door, still wearing her apron. Becca watched her go through the screen door, wondering if she should tell her and if Jill would even care. She laughed to herself when she walked back to the workbench, reached for the piping bags —and smashed right up against the cake in the process.

White hot fear gripped her as her eyes widened in horror. She opened her mouth but no sound escaped.

No! No, no, no, no!

She tried to process what had happened, dared to even think that somehow she could turn back time, just a few seconds. That somehow, she could have avoided this disaster.

But it had happened. The beautiful cake was ruined. All of their hard work was destroyed.

For a moment she thought it would be okay, that maybe when she pulled back the cake wouldn't be as bad as she feared, that maybe she could just smooth out the side, and the flowers would remain intact. But then she slowly inched away, seeing the mix of colors on her apron, the beautiful, carefully finished cake now a huge mess.

As her heart pounded against her chest, she tried to come up with a plan. A fast one.

She'd have to refrost it. She could do that! But then she saw that the bowl containing the carefully colored buttercream was on the drying rack—and that several of the carefully piped flowers were now smeared on her apron, a blur of color.

She looked at the clock, calculating how long it would take to finish, wrestling with whether or not she should call Jill back into the kitchen.

But no, Jill was picking up the flowers. And Carly was in charge of Daisy.

And that left only one other person with a set of capable hands.

She plucked her phone from her apron pocket and stared at the dark screen. She hesitated, thinking that she could just do it herself, but deep down knowing that she couldn't. Not with the clock ticking away the minutes until the wedding.

And Jonah did say he wanted to help with the wedding.

Before she could change her mind, she pulled up his name from her contacts list. He picked up on the first ring.

"I need you," she said. If it weren't for such a pressing disaster, she'd almost have to laugh at the irony of her words. And maybe she would. But not today.

When Becca called, Jonah had assumed it was to tell him an update about the storefront next door, but it was clear from her tone that she hadn't heard from Denise yet.

That the space next door was currently the furthest thing from her mind.

"I won't even have a bakery to come back to on Monday if my sisters see this! They'll fire me if they don't kill me first!" came her panicked voice.

Jonah was already in his car before she'd ended the call, pushing back the rush he felt that she'd reached out to him.

She must have been as desperate as she sounded. Or maybe, he dared to think, there was hope yet. Not just for the restaurant. But for them too.

He let himself in through the back kitchen door to find Becca standing at the far counter, mixing up the buttercream, a line of food coloring bottles beside her.

She turned then, revealing a three-tiered wedding cake that looked like a child had eagerly rubbed their hands all over one side, and he had to cover his mouth to stop from laughing. And even then he failed. Miserably.

"What happened to this cake?" Jonah stared at the smeared middle tier, and the top part of the bottom, too.

"It's not funny," she said, pushing a strand of hair from her forehead with the back of her hand. Her cheeks were flushed and her eyes were bright, but he thought he saw her shoulders relax at the sight of him.

"It's only funny because I know we can fix it." When she didn't match his smile, he said, "Come on. You know this is a story you'll be telling your grandkids someday."

He felt the grin slip from his own face. This was the way they used to talk, imagining a future, a shared one. Now he wondered if he'd ever have kids of his own. Becca might.

There was no reason why she wouldn't settle down with some lucky guy.

A guy who hadn't turned his back on her.

He picked up a piping bag. "It's been a while since I've used one of these. I hope it's like riding a bike."

"There are some things that even time can't erase." She glanced up at him and then away. "We'd better work quickly. Frankie is picking up the cake soon and I still have to get showered and dressed."

"You trust Frankie to carry this cake over to Concetti's?" Jonah piped one flower. Becca was right; it did come back easily.

"More than I trust myself right now. And if you did it, Maria might shove it back onto your shirt."

He laughed, but he knew it was entirely possible. It would take time to win over Maria's affection again. To get her to trust him. Know his intentions.

Maybe that's all it would take with Becca, too. Time.

"Guess people see me as the bad guy around here," he said.

Becca added another dot of food coloring to the large bowl and stirred it until it was a near-perfect match to the yellow buttercream that covered the cake.

"Not everyone." She gave him a little smile. "Ah, a perfect match!" Becca's grin was full of satisfaction when she started patching the frosting. "See? Sometimes things do work out. Even when it feels like all hope is lost."

He stared at her for a moment and then picked up his piping bag again. He wanted to believe that.

But he just didn't see how they could ever find a way to have everything they both wanted. And each other.

The cake looked so perfect by the time they finished that Becca didn't see the need to mention the mishap to Jill. She left Jonah to guard the cake and wait for Frankie and then hurried home to shower and do her hair and makeup before meeting her sisters at Nana's house.

Daisy was the first to greet her, already wearing her flower girl dress, all too happy to flaunt her pink-painted nails.

"You'll be prettier than the bride!" Becca told her.

But as soon as she saw her grandmother, she knew that wasn't possible. Nana came down the hallway, her hair in curlers, her makeup not yet applied, wearing the same old bathrobe that she used to when she'd peek through the space in the dining room curtains, watching when Jonah would drop her off after a date, yet somehow she'd never looked prettier than in this moment.

There was something different about her, something that must have been missing, all these years. A light in her eyes. A flush in her cheeks.

"You look beautiful, Nana," Becca said, giving her a long hug.

"Please." Nana waved away the compliment. "I'm just about to start getting ready."

Becca watched the old woman walk up the stairs lined with framed photos, still life captures of time gone by, but she had a lightness in her step of a young girl, much like the faded, black and white photo of Nana holding Becca's mother on her lap.

Becca swallowed hard against the image when she saw Carly come into the hallway from the kitchen, reminding Daisy to be careful in her dress.

"Doesn't Nana look different somehow?" Becca said. "There's something in her eyes. It's hard to say what it is."

Carly gave a little smile. "It's hope."

Yes, that was it. Nana might have been satisfied with her life, even found joy again after such deep losses, but for the first time in a long time, she was looking to the future.

While Becca's felt just as uncertain as ever.

"Well, the limousine should be here in a couple of hours." Carly checked her watch. "I'll be watching out the window to be sure Robert and Jonah have already left for the church before we venture outside."

Becca laughed. "You really think there's any chance of bad luck happening at this wedding?"

If there was then hopefully she'd gotten it out of the way by nearly destroying the cake. And even then, she'd managed to fix the damage. Turn the day around.

Thanks to Jonah.

Carly considered this for a moment and then shrugged. "Maybe I'm just being silly. Or carried away with all this romance."

Becca nodded, pushing aside all thoughts of Jonah rushing to her aid this morning. Surely that was all it was. It was a wedding day. Who couldn't feel a little sentimental?

And by the time the car pulled up outside the church in

the center of town, Becca was feeling just that. Here they were, three sisters in beautiful blue gowns, Daisy, clutching Carly's hand, and Nana, holding her bouquet.

Three generations under one roof, but from the faraway look that passed over Nana's eyes, Becca knew that, like all of them, Nana was probably thinking about the missing generation.

"If Mom were here, I think I'd know what she'd tell you," Jill said, taking Nana's hand.

"About time?" Carly joked, lightening the mood. It was no secret that their mother had encouraged Nana to date after her husband passed.

"That you look beautiful," Jill said, flashing Carly a stern glance.

"And happy," Becca added. "But then, they go hand in hand."

"I used to think that moving on to the next chapter meant closing the door on my last." Nana looked them each in the eye. "Now I see that sometimes, somehow, you really can have it all."

Becca smiled sadly, knowing this was true for her grandmother, but wondering if she would ever be able to say the same for herself.

"I think the guests have finished taking their seats." Carly stared out the tinted windows. "Daisy and I will go inside and give you the all-clear."

"I'll stay with you Nana," Jill said.

Becca felt the emotions rising in her throat, and she struggled to blink back tears.

"We've come a long way," she managed to say. "You most of all, Nana."

"Not just me," Nana insisted. "All of us. Though I will say I can't believe I'm actually getting married again. It's funny, I'm far from young, but I can't help but feel like suddenly I have my whole life before me."

"Love will do that to a person," Carly said, putting an arm around Daisy.

With one last glance at her grandmother, Becca stepped out of the car, following Carly and Daisy up the steps. Inside, the guests were seated, evenly divided between the bride's and groom's sides, though few in this town would ever be as beloved as Nana Parker. Nick's mother was playing the piano, and Robert Quincy was already standing at the altar.

Becca stepped away from the door, about to run outside and wave to the car, when she saw Jonah coming around the corner.

In a black tux and white tie, he looked exactly as she'd once envisioned him on their wedding day. Only in that fantasy, she was the one hiding in the car, not wanting to risk any bad luck, and she'd only have her first glimpse of him when she began her wedding march.

He hesitated for a moment, then stuck his hands in his pockets and gave her a slow grin. Her breath caught as she watched him approach, giving her an appreciative once-over.

"You look beautiful," he said softly, his gaze locking on hers.

For a moment, it felt like they were all alone, but all too soon Daisy started begging Carly to let her start to walk down the aisle and Becca could tell that Nick's mother was nearing the end of her current song.

"You should probably take your place," she told him. "We don't want to keep the guests—or Daisy—waiting much longer."

"Or my grandfather," Jonah agreed with a quirk of his mouth, but still, he didn't show any signs of moving.

"My grandmother did only make the poor man wait about a decade," Becca laughed.

"Some things are worth waiting for," Jonah said. Then, after a pause: "The best things."

She swallowed hard. "Well, you'd better get out there then."

"I suppose so." He kept his gaze on her. "Here I was thinking we were going to finally have a chance to walk down the aisle together."

Becca's heart thudded straight into her gut. "Guess it wasn't meant to be," she managed.

His eyes turned a little flat. "Not this time."

Becca wasn't sure what he meant by that or if she even wanted to know, but now wasn't the time to be thinking of herself, anyway. The ceremony was starting. Jonah was walking down the aisle, taking his place beside his grandfather, and now Daisy was getting ready to go next.

Becca hurried to the church doors and waved frantically to the car, where Jill was looking up out the half-open window.

Stepping back inside, she looked at her sister. "I think we're almost ready."

"Remember, just one flower at a time," Carly whispered to Daisy. "You have to make them last."

Daisy nodded soberly, her expression so serious that Becca almost wondered if she'd dare to crack a smile, but then the music swelled and Carly gave her a little nudge of encouragement and Daisy lit up, dropping petals a little quicker than she'd been instructed, all to the oohs and awes of the onlookers. By the time she reached her father in the front row, she'd long run out of flowers.

Carly took a breath as Jill and Nana came through the door. "I guess that means I'm next!"

Next down the aisle, and probably not just today, Becca thought. Like Nana, Carly had found the missing piece of her life, years after she'd stopped searching.

Jill leaned in over Becca's shoulder and said, "You doing okay?"

Becca swallowed against her emotions and nodded firmly. She couldn't admit that she wasn't so sure she was okay at all. That once, she'd imagined walking down the aisle to Jonah, standing at the altar. Only in that dream, she'd been the bride and this had been their wedding day.

Clutching the bouquet in her hand, she began the march steadily after Carly, focusing on the friends and neighbors who all looked on with smiles, some, like Maria, with tears of happiness.

She could see Jonah to her right, up ahead, in her periphery, and she tried to keep him there, on the fringes, not at her center, just as she'd tried for all these weeks that he'd been back in town and, before that, for the years after he had left.

The pull grew stronger as she approached Carly, no

longer directly in front of her but now taking her position, off to the side, exchanging less than subtle glances with Nick and Daisy. Mr. Quincy looked happier than she'd seen him in months—if not years—and Becca knew she should leave it at that. Find joy in someone else's happiness. And she did.

But when her eyes met Jonah's as she scooted into position, there was something else there, too. A wish, perhaps. For what might have been.

For a promise that had been broken.

His grin broadened as their eyes met and she gave him a little smile, aware that there was an audience and that the last thing Nana deserved was to have every eye in Hope Hollow analyzing the body language between her and Jonah.

This was Nana's day. Someday, somehow, she might have her own.

But it wouldn't be with Jonah.

No, that hadn't been meant to be.

Concetti's had been transformed from a cozy, candlelit restaurant into an elegant space. The tables were pushed together to form long banquettes, anchored by votive candles and small centerpieces. There was enough pasta to feed the town and the next one over, and the cake that rested on its own table, away from elbows or other possible accidents, showed no evidence of what had happened this morning.

"I'd say we did a pretty good job," Becca said to Jonah now, as he came to stand beside her, clearly having noticed that she was carefully inspecting it, even if from a safe distance.

"I'd say we make a pretty good team," he countered, raising his glass to her.

They did, when they wanted to, and for today she'd leave it at that. She shifted her eyes back to the cake and then over to the dance floor.

"The band is excellent," Becca made a point of saying. She studied his face for a moment. "Was it worth the trip to the site of your parents' old restaurant?"

Jonah nodded. "I've always been afraid to really face my past, but I'm glad I did. And I think my grandfather is too."

She followed his gaze to where Nana and Robert were dancing, a circle of onlookers slowly joining them, all too aware of Jonah's warm presence beside her, and the fact that they were amongst the few not swaying to the music.

"Are we dancing?" Jonah asked, breaking the ice.

It was a wedding, after all. One that meant that Jonah was going to be a part of her life whether she wanted him to or not. And like she'd come to realize over the past few weeks, it was far easier to let Jonah back in than to resist him.

"We never did get our wedding dance," he said, giving her a hopeful look.

She tipped her head. "Are we there yet? Making light of the wedding that never happened?"

"Would it be so wrong to say that some days I wish it had?" he asked, his voice husky as his eyes locked with hers.

Her heart was pounding, and she stared at him, not knowing what to say, think, or even believe.

She only knew what she wanted. To dance with him. To hold him close. Even if it was just one more time.

"You did brave that awful diner to track down this band," she said.

He set his wineglass on the nearest table. "Is that a yes?"

"Let's just say you earned it," she sighed as they moved closer to the dance floor.

"I think we both did," he said as he stepped in front of her.

She froze in place as he reached out a hand, sliding it over her waist, his fingers tightening their grip on the fabric of her dress as he pulled her closer. His other hand reached for hers, and she pressed herself against his chest, her chin at his shoulder, feeling his breath in her ear. Her heart hammered in her chest, and she wondered if he could feel it beating against his own.

If, like her, this moment felt complicated. So right. And yet so difficult.

Nothing had changed between them in their two years apart. And that was just the problem.

Across the room, she caught Maria's eyebrow lift and Jill's small frown. They were just being protective, she knew. Denise, however, seemed to beam from where she sat at her table, sipping a glass of champagne.

"Everyone's watching us," Jonah whispered in her ear. The heat of his breath against her skin sent a shiver through her as she broke away from his arms.

"This isn't our night," she said, swallowing hard as she looked up into his eyes, thinking of how it might have been. Could have been.

Should have been.

But tonight was about Nana and Robert. The attention should be only on them.

Jonah nudged his chin toward the door. "Want to take a walk?

She hesitated. Most of the town seemed to be crammed into the space. No one would notice if they disappeared for a few minutes. Some fresh air would be nice if only to clear her head.

"Think Mamma Maria has forgiven me yet?" he asked once they were alone on the sidewalk. It was a cool night; the warmer ones wouldn't hit until deeper into the summer months, and the moon was full, its light bright.

"She has been known to hold a grudge," Becca reminded him. "Remember that girl that Frankie brought home?"

"Which one?" Jonah laughed. "The one who said she didn't like cheese on pizza or the one who said she didn't eat carbs?"

"There was recently one who cut her spaghetti." Becca was laughing too.

"Oh, I missed that!" Jonah looked sincerely disappointed when he stuffed his hands into his pockets and let out a sigh. "I feel like I've missed a lot."

"You never visited," Becca pointed out.

"It was hard to get away. The hours at the restaurant were long and I used up the few vacation days I had for stupid things, like work around the apartment, or sick days."

"Sounds as grueling as the bakery," Becca only half-joked. "With Nana gone, it was one less set of hands for a while. Now Carly's back but somehow the work still never stops."

"It's easy to get lost in something you love," Jonah said. He slid her a glance. "Easy to forget to prioritize who you love."

She pulled in a breath as he turned to face her, opening his mouth to start to speak. From the look in his eyes, to apologize. But they'd said enough, hurt enough, drudged up the past enough.

And right now, all she wanted to think about was this moment. Not yesterday. Not tomorrow. Just...today.

He bent to kiss her, wrapping his arms around her waist, and pulling her close against his chest. She relaxed into him, to the taste and feel of him, to that one thing that had always felt so certain in her life...until it wasn't.

She backed up, touching her lips. Jonah was frowning at her, looking confused, but then his mouth spread into a grin, and despite all her reservations, she smiled too.

They'd never be able to undo the past. They'd always have to live with it. But maybe there was a place for it—and them—in the future.

If she was open to it.

He took her hand, and she didn't pull it back, as they slowly strolled down the quiet Main Street, until they came to stop in front of the storefront, the one that had once displayed beautiful wedding gowns in the front window, always fresh, usually seasonal. Once, so inspiring, reminding Becca of her upcoming nuptials every time she left the bakery until eventually, it started becoming a reminder of something that had never happened.

Or maybe, something that she'd let slip away.

"Well, it's the wedding day," Jonah said as they stood side by side, staring into the darkened space, their reflections barely visible in the glass.

"Denise will probably make a decision soon," Becca said, nodding.

"If she hasn't already," Jonah said.

Becca considered that, knowing that Denise was back at the party right now, and they could probably ask her, together.

But knowing would change things.

And she wasn't so ready for that just yet.

thirteen

It was another normal day at the bakery, and Sundays were notoriously busy. Even though many people from town had stayed out late the night before celebrating the new bride and groom, the usual customers started filing through the door in search of their coffee, scones, and muffins as soon as Becca turned the sign.

"You must not have slept at all last night!" Erika remarked, pushing her younger son's hands from reaching for the muffin that Becca had just set down on the counter.

It was true that Becca had barely slept last night, but probably not for the reasons that Erika suspected.

She wasn't tired yet, but she knew by the time the afternoon crowd hit that she'd be fighting fatigue even coffee couldn't cure. For now, she was content to bask in the sweet memories of a perfect evening. A beautiful wedding. A wonderful community.

An unexpected kiss with Jonah.

She pulled in a breath, hoping to silence those butterflies

that seemed to flutter every time she remembered the feel of his mouth on hers.

"I didn't," she admitted. "But then, that's what weddings are for, right?"

"Oh, I wasn't talking about the wedding." Erika was momentarily distracted by her older son, who was now arguing with his brother about which muffin looked bigger. She grabbed the two plates, marched them to the nearest table, cut both baked goods in half, and swapped them.

Erika rolled her eyes skyward as she walked back to the counter, but she was smiling. "It isn't even eight in the morning and already they're a handful. Can I make that an extra-large coffee today?"

"Of course." Becca was happy for the task, and hoped that Erika's children might have distracted her from whatever she had planned to say. Had someone witnessed their kiss last night? They had been standing on Main Street, for anyone to see, even though most people were enjoying the music back at Concetti's.

She really didn't want to be the talk of the town again. She just wanted... She stopped as she popped the lid onto the paper cup. She supposed she just wanted what she'd always wanted.

A simple, quiet life, doing what she loved, here in this town. With the man she loved.

Her stomach swooped and soared a little as she handed Erika the coffee. "This should help."

"Thanks," Erika took it gratefully. But instead of reaching for her wallet, she tipped her head. "So you really haven't heard yet?"

Now Becca realized with dread that Erika wasn't talking about the kiss at all.

"Did Denise make a decision?" Maybe this time, Erika really was here to deliver the verdict.

"Not that I know of, but her decision just got a little easier." Erika paused to frown. "You didn't know that Jonah pulled his bid?"

Becca stared at Erika, unable to hide her shock. Suddenly, replaying last night was no longer about the kiss at all, but everything that had been said before and after it.

"Pulled his bid? No, I didn't know. He..." He'd never so much as hinted at such a thing. "But...why?"

"I don't know," Erika shrugged. "He mentioned it to me yesterday when he asked me to list the house."

"The house?" Just when Becca thought her shock couldn't be greater, it was. "Which house?" Even though there was only one she could think of, it didn't make sense. He'd just moved back. Just told her that he'd be living in the house next door to Nana's.

He had a plan.

But his plans, it would seem, had once again changed.

"His grandfather's house," Erika confirmed. "I'm going over there this morning to put up the sign."

Becca managed to shake her head, but her mind felt fuzzy, and she didn't even know what to say.

"I...didn't know," she repeated.

But then, it would seem that she didn't know a lot of things about Jonah—only that for the second time, he'd made plans. Lots of them. Ones that didn't include her.

Breaking away from the bakery early wasn't an option. The door kept opening, people kept ordering, and most stopped to chat and tell Becca and her sisters how much they enjoyed last night's festivities.

"Your grandmother was a beautiful bride," Debbie from the flower shop said. "And that cake was so beautiful! You girls are so talented."

"It was a team effort." Becca's stomach pulled on the memory of Jonah's words. "But the credit really goes to Jill," she added.

Just then Denise appeared behind Debbie, who turned to her with a huge smile. "Oh, Denise! I was just talking about the wedding. That dress couldn't have been more perfect for our Sharon."

Becca nodded in agreement. It was true. It was just the right amount of understated elegance that most people came to associate with the woman who had been a pillar of the community for most of her life.

"Well, I'd better get back to the shop. I often see an uptick in business after a big wedding. Puts the idea of romance into the air." Debbie waved as she hurried off, leaving Becca face-to-face with Denise.

"What will it be this morning?" Becca fought against the nerves that fluttered in her stomach.

"I'm actually not here for any treats this morning," Denise said slowly.

Becca wasn't surprised. Denise had said she'd give her

answer after the wedding, and she was a woman of integrity. "Did you...make your decision?"

With Jonah out of the running, that meant it was between her and the third offer—and she still didn't know any of the details on that. Her heart was thumping with anticipation and dread. That something she'd wanted might finally happen.

But at what cost?

Denise nodded. "I have made my decision, and it wasn't an easy one." She let out a small sigh and Becca knew then and there. The news wasn't good.

"I've decided to keep the shop," Denise said firmly.

Becca realized that she had been expecting a no, but not for this reason. "Keep the shop?"

Denise leaned into the counter, her words coming out in rush. "Working on your grandmother's wedding dress and seeing her walk down the aisle looking so beautiful in it reminded me how much I love what I do. And that I don't think I'm ready to give it all up just yet." She reached out and squeezed Becca's hand. "I'm so sorry. I know you had your hopes up."

Becca stared at the woman, a strange sense of relief filling her chest. "I did. I mean, we would have loved to expand the bakery, but we're also content with what we have here. This place is special. Just like yours." She gave Denise an encouraging smile. "You really did make my grandmother happy with that dress."

"It's nice to be a part of someone's most special day," Denise agreed. "But then, you must feel that way too. Every time you make a wedding cake."

It was true, only recently, Becca hadn't felt that way. She'd gotten away from the joy of that part of her job. From the heart of it. Somewhere along the way, it became about holding on to something, instead of remembering why she'd started in the first place.

That it wasn't about bigger or better or even the bottom line. It was about carrying on family traditions. Keeping a part of her mother with her. Sharing that love that she'd been lucky to have ever known.

"Well," Denise was saying. "I should go before the line builds up."

"Can I ask you something?" Becca stopped her. "Did… you already tell Jonah? About your decision?"

"Jonah? No. I had a missed call from the real estate agent this morning but I haven't had a chance to listen to it yet. I suppose everyone was waiting for my decision and I wanted to tell you in person. I did promise to have it made by the wedding, and yesterday only confirmed my decision. Going through the process these past couple of weeks really reminded me of what I love and why I do it." She looked at Becca coyly. "But then, you probably understand that, too."

Becca swallowed hard. There was no sense dismissing Denise's less-than-subtle implication. She had been reminded of what she loved these past couple of weeks, but more than that, who she loved.

But if Jonah hadn't put his house on the market because he knew Denise had unlisted the space next door, then what was his reason?

~

Becca waited until they'd closed for the day—early, as they were known to do on Sundays—and her sisters were both in the kitchen to break the news. She knew they were expecting it, and they'd all probably secretly considered this outcome—even Carly, who always found a way to hold out hope.

"Well, there's no easy way to say this, but we are not going to be getting the space next door after all."

Her sisters both stared at her, silently digesting this information. Jill was the first to give a nod, but Carly gave a sad smile.

"I have to admit that I'm a little relieved," she admitted.

"You?" Jill shot her a look. "But you were the one who pushed for this!"

"I did," Carly agreed. "But the more it became a possibility, the more I began to doubt things. I know we've changed the bakery recently, adding new recipes and sprucing up the front room, but...I don't like the idea of changing it too much. If we expanded, it would all feel different. Maybe, too different."

Becca felt a smile grow on her own face. "I feel the same way." A bigger kitchen had its perks, but a new space wouldn't be the same one where she'd learned to knead dough or make her mother's favorite cookies.

There had been a time when Becca thought she might someday have her own children, ones she would bring to this kitchen to learn the simple joys that she had inherited.

Had she given up on that dream? Or just thought she could replace it with something better?

"Then why didn't you speak up?" Jill asked them both, astonished.

"Because I thought you both wanted this!" Becca said. "And Carly had a point. This might have been our only opportunity."

"And I would have been content keeping things the same, too," Jill said. "I was only convinced we should try so that Jonah couldn't sweep in and take anything more from you."

"Does that mean that Jonah's going to be opening his restaurant next door?" Carly asked. It was clear from her tone and expression that she wasn't sure how she should react to this.

"Actually, Denise has decided to move back in."

"She's reopening the dress shop?" Carly blinked, but then a flush of pink spread over her cheeks. "I have to admit that I'm not unhappy about this. She makes beautiful wedding gowns."

"Are you in the market for one?" Jill asked pertly, causing a deeper blush to rise up on their youngest sister's face.

"No. At least, not yet." She smiled. "But what about you?" she asked Becca.

Becca barked out a laugh. "Me? My wedding planning days are behind me."

"I meant, what about you and Jonah?" Carly pressed.

"There is no me and Jonah," Becca said flatly, getting back to work. She pulled some dough that had risen from the proving drawer and scooped it onto the workbench.

Her sisters were watching her carefully as she began kneading the dough the way her mother had taught her, on this very counter. Her hands were small then, dimpled at the knuckles, but her mother's hands were long and lean.

Like her own were now. She pushed back those emotions. Thinking of how close she'd come to holding on to something so tightly that she'd lost sight of the heart of it. Of what really mattered.

Of what she really wanted.

"I thought that you and Jonah were getting along better these past few weeks," Jill observed.

"We were." Becca couldn't argue with that. "But only because we wanted Nana's wedding to be a success. Now it's over."

And so was whatever she and Jonah had started to have. Or maybe it was over before it even began. Long over. Over the day that Jonah took that job in California.

Or maybe the day that she decided not to go with him. To hold on so tightly to her past that she lost sight of what her heart needed most.

"Jonah's apparently listing his grandfather's house," she told her sisters. "He's not going to be living there after all."

Carly stared at her, sharing her confusion. "Where's he going to live then?"

Becca tried to shrug off her hurt but there was no use. "Beats me. He must have a plan."

"Let me guess? One he made on his own again?" Jill tsked her disapproval, and Becca appreciated the camaraderie.

No matter how tough things got, she always had this kitchen, this bakery, and her sisters. Most days, it was enough. But some days, she couldn't help but feel the emptiness in that part of her heart that had once been filled by Jonah.

And she'd been foolish enough to let him slide right back in these past few weeks.

"Well, Jonah isn't the only one moving," Carly said. "Now that Robert's moved in, it's time for me to move out. I've already packed. And I'm more than a little grateful that they decided to spend their wedding night at the Hope Hollow Inn last night."

Becca managed to laugh. "We're ready to welcome you and help you unpack." It would be good to have Carly with them. A new dynamic. Another voice to fill the silence.

"I'm moving in with Nick, actually." Carly looked at each of them nervously. "It will be easier with Daisy, and it will give us a chance to spend more time together. And to be honest, I don't think I can stomach one more accidental interruption of Nana and—"

"Stop!" Jill held up a hand, her cheeks as red as the strawberries she was slicing.

"You and Nick are really close," Becca observed, giving her sister a smile. "I'm really happy for you, Carly."

And she was. Nana and Carly had both had their fair share of heartache in life. Maybe it was necessary in order to know true love. To appreciate it. And hold on to it.

"Well, now that the fate of the bakery has been determined, my love life is settled, and Nana is far from bored in her retirement, that only leaves the two of you to worry about." Carly gave them both a pert look.

"There's nothing to worry about over here," Jill said firmly.

Becca couldn't agree or disagree. There was nothing to

worry about, though, that much was true. And that in itself was a gift.

"After the year we've been through, it will be nice to have a little less drama," Becca said with a sigh. "Now we can settle into our new routine, enjoy what we have, and stop wishing for more."

Carly gave her a look across the counter that said she wasn't buying it. "You're too young to be this complacent," she said.

Becca shook her head. "I'm not like you, Carly. I never was. I've always been happy right here, in this kitchen, even when I was making Nana's recipes."

"But isn't it more fun to create some of your own?" Carly countered.

Her sister had her there. But there was something special about honoring the past too.

"I'm just saying that there's been a lot of...uncertainty. And change. And now everything's sort of fallen into place. It's all worked out in the end."

"Has it?" Carly replied, raising an eyebrow.

"Are you talking about Jonah?" Becca asked, even though she already knew the answer.

"I'm just saying that maybe you should talk to him. Maybe it's worth a try."

There was that word again. A part of her wanted to tell her sister that it was no use, that Jonah had made up his mind and there was no stopping him. That they wanted different things—or things that conflicted with each other's needs. That he'd already made his choice.

But the other part of her remembered how she'd felt

when he'd left the last time. How a part of her had lived with doubt that crept in when she least expected it. That she hadn't tried to stop him, but instead just let him go.

And that maybe she was doing the same thing all over again.

fourteen

Becca waited until the following day to visit her grandmother. This time she rang the doorbell first, and her eyes kept darting to the for-sale sign in front of the house next door while she waited. Jonah's car wasn't in the driveway, and she hadn't heard from him since their kiss on Saturday night.

Maybe he'd already left town. Maybe this time it was easier than saying goodbye.

"Becca?" Nana stared at her in confusion after she opened the door. "Why didn't you just let yourself in?"

Becca blushed. "Oh, you know...it's different now, since it's Mr. Quincy's house, too. I mean, Robert."

"Nonsense." Nana clucked her tongue and closed the door behind Becca. "This will always be your home and there's always room for more family, too."

"If you're insinuating that Jonah and I might get back together, that's not going to happen."

"Why would you think I'd be insinuating that?" Nana blinked in mock innocence.

"I think we both know that your fondness toward Jonah isn't entirely on account of him being Robert's only grandson." Becca gave her grandmother a knowing look.

Nana bristled as she led Becca past the dining room, whose table was covered in wedding gifts still waiting to be opened, to the kitchen where a pie was cooling on a rack.

If Jill were here, she'd be scolding Nana about her arthritis, but Becca couldn't help but smile. Baking was a part of Nana's soul. She should never have to give up what she loved.

It was something she'd told herself, many times over the two years after Jonah left. That he'd made her choose between what she loved and whom she loved.

But maybe he'd made that choice for her. He'd said he knew she wouldn't follow him to California. And he'd gone anyway.

"How do you feel about Carly moving out?" Becca asked as she helped Nana prepare tea.

"Oh, I'll miss her, but she won't be far this time. It was nice having a chance to reconnect with her these past couple of months, but it's important for her to think about her future, too."

Becca filled the teapot. "Yes, I guess that's probably something I should do too."

Her grandmother set a hand on her shoulder before taking the teapot from her and setting it on the stovetop.

"I know that you're disappointed about not being able to expand the bakery," Nana commented. "Carly told us the news when we came home last evening."

Becca gave a little shrug. "I'm not as disappointed as I thought I'd be. It seemed exciting at first, but in the end, I like my life the way that it is."

"You sure about that?"

Becca thought about it and then gave her grandmother a half-smile. "I thought I was fine with things the way they are—going to work every day, with my sisters, in a bakery that has been in the family for generations, doing what I was meant to do. What I love. But when I started to think that there might be...more to life, the recent news did leave me feeling a little...empty, I suppose."

Nana sighed. "Jonah has always had a restless soul, Becca. That doesn't mean his feelings for you weren't true."

Becca swallowed hard, willing herself not to cry. She'd shed enough tears for Jonah, then and now. When would she learn her lesson?

"You know he loves you," Nana said softly.

Becca stayed quiet. Loves, not loved. She supposed she did know that, even when she'd tried to fight it. Even when she'd tried to deny it in herself.

"But not enough." Becca sighed. "Or maybe I don't love him enough."

"Sometimes it isn't about love at all." Nana paused. "Answer me this. If Jonah hadn't gone to California, where would that have left the two of you?"

Becca didn't need to think about the answer. He wouldn't have gotten the space next to the bakery, meaning even now, he'd still be waiting for that dream to come true.

"He'd probably have always wondered what might have been." Maybe, even resented staying.

"Life is about choice. For so long, I had my mind made up not to give Robert a chance. Then one day, Carly convinced me to try. And look at me now." Nana beamed.

"You're saying that I should give up everything that matters so much to me?"

Nana sighed. "I'm saying that you should give him a chance. It may lead nowhere. And then you'd be right back where you are now. Brokenhearted. Or it could lead somewhere wonderful. You'll never know unless—"

"Don't say it," Becca groaned. "Besides, he's moving."

"I know." Nana didn't show any further reaction. But of course, she would have known. The sign was up, and it was still Robert's house.

"Well, I hope that you don't intend to put this house on the market too," Becca said, eager to get off the topic of Jonah for a minute, and suddenly alarmed at the thought of her childhood home being taken away. "I imagine you and your new husband will want to have all sorts of adventures now that you have the time and a person to share with it."

"Oh, we don't need to travel to find happiness," Nana told her. "We have everything we love right here in Hope Hollow. What more could we find outside of this community?"

Becca relaxed, but then she wondered if Jonah would ever see it the same way. He'd been searching all his life for something to replace the one thing he'd lost, and he might never find it.

A part of her that once loved him, and maybe still did, couldn't help but feel sad about that.

"Speaking of which, I still have to pick up Robert's wedding gift." Nana checked her watch.

"What did you get him?" Becca asked conversationally. An engraved watch, perhaps?

"A puppy," Nana replied.

Becca looked at her sharply, waiting for the punchline to the joke, and then, realizing that her grandmother was serious, she started laughing.

"You got him a puppy?" She stared at her grandmother, waiting for that glint in her eyes to appear, only to find that it didn't. They'd begged their grandmother for a dog when they were little, only to be ever told that it wouldn't be fair to them or the dog, considering how much time the family spent at the bakery. "You do realize that since you're living together, that means it will be your dog too?"

Her grandmother smiled widely. "I know. And I can't think of anything that would make Robert or me happier than to know his heart is whole again. Besides, I think it will be nice to have some new energy in the house. I never made time for a dog before and I always loved animals. But then, I didn't make time for a lot of things."

Becca fell silent, knowing it was true, and not just for her grandmother.

Just like Nana, she'd poured everything into the bakery. Let it fill the parts of her that she'd lost along the way.

But now she was beginning to think of everything she'd lost out on just the same.

Jonah was stepping out of his car when Becca left the house, now wishing she'd tagged along with Nana to pick up the puppy, even though she'd probably spared herself from coming home with one of her own.

She stopped on the flagstone path, but it was too late. He'd seen her and was now walking toward her. His hands were thrust into the pocket of his jeans, and he looked nervous as she hardened her stare on him.

"I was just thinking of you," he said, and now Becca really stopped to frown.

"Funny, I assumed you hadn't thought of me at all." She motioned to the sign in the yard. "I thought you were planning on staying here."

"Change of plans."

"When were you planning to tell me you're moving?" Before he could reply, she added, "I mean, my grandmother and sister do live next door, so they were bound to see the sign."

"It all happened so fast," Jonah explained. "I was going to tell you."

"After you decided to pull your bid on the store?"

His brow furrowed in confusion. "I thought you'd be happy about that—"

"Denise is keeping the space for herself," Becca replied.

Jonah looked so genuinely disappointed, that for a moment she wondered if he'd done it for her. But just as quickly, the sign caught her eye again, reminding her of the cold facts.

"I suppose you had a backup plan all along," she said a little bitterly.

"Not all along," he replied, seeming surprised by her reaction. "Just…recently."

She pursed her lips. Of course. A contingency plan. A safety net. A better option.

"I'm sorry you didn't get the space," he said, moving toward her, causing her to take a step back. "I know…I know how much you wanted it. What it meant to you."

She looked at him with fresh hurt. "I'm not sure you ever understood what that bakery means to me. What family means to me."

"That's not fair," he said firmly, his eyes hardening.

Maybe it wasn't, but she needed to make it clear if only to make him understand why she hadn't followed him to California. Why she'd let him go.

"You and I both know what it's like to lose our parents," she said quietly. "That bakery was the last happy memory of my mother. Those recipes keep her alive, Jonah. Every day I stand in the kitchen she once stood in, seeing her photo on the wall, working at the same counter where she taught me how to ice a cake. I can't let that go. Not now. Not ever. Because it would be like letting go of the last part of her."

"I never expected you to," he said. His eyes were so pleading that she had no choice but to believe him, but that didn't change a damn thing, did it?

"So you were just willing to let me go then?"

He pulled in a breath and shook his head. "You were the only thing keeping me here, Becca. You and my grandfather, but you both had other things in your life. And I had this… need. This unfilled dream. And it was starting to feel like it would never come true."

"Then why pull your bid on the space now?" she asked. "Why give up before knowing the outcome?"

"Because," he said slowly. "I had a change of heart."

She stared at him, for the second time in her life wondering how it was possible that he could give up on a dream he'd wanted so badly.

"But you only ever wanted—"

"You," he said softly, his eyes searching hers. "I wasn't going to hurt you again, Becca."

"Don't tell me you pulled your bid because of me," she said, her breath locking in her chest. Without that space, he had nothing to keep him in town. The for sale sign on his yard was proof of that.

"These past couple of weeks reminded me of what we had. What we could still have. Of the life that I walked away from. The dream. I still want that dream, Becca. And I want you to have yours too."

"So what are you saying?" she asked, needing to hear that he wasn't going anywhere. That this time, it would all work out somehow.

"When I pulled my bid, I hoped that you would get the space." He looked so disappointed by the outcome that she knew it was true.

She stared at him, something in her stomach dropping when she remembered that more was coming. "But your restaurant—"

He held up his palms, giving her a slow, pleased smile. "I found another location. A better location."

And there it was.

She shook her head, blinking back tears at what a fool

she'd been to think that things might be different this time around. "So you made your own plans and thought you could tell me about it later."

He frowned at her as he pulled back. "I didn't intend it like that, but yes. I thought—I thought you'd be happy for me. You know I've always wanted my own place, and this spot on Main Street was never going to be mine."

"You don't know for sure that Denise wouldn't have chosen you over me," Becca said, wondering for a moment what might have been if she hadn't been so determined to have it, just because it was right next door to the bakery. Just because it kept him from being so close.

She'd wanted to keep him distant, even when he'd come back.

To hold on to the past, even the worst parts of it.

"It wasn't meant to be mine," he said, sounding resigned, but not disappointed.

"Maybe none of this was meant to be," she said.

"What's that supposed to mean?" he asked, frowning.

She tossed up her hands in exasperation. "You and me, Jonah. Nothing has changed. We both put our ambitions first, again. We made the same choices, for the second time."

"I don't think that," he said. "It's not that straight-forward."

No, because nothing with him was.

"And that kiss Saturday night? Did that mean anything to you at all?"

"Of course it did." Jonah stepped toward her. "I didn't think you'd give me a second chance."

"Well, maybe I shouldn't have," she said, backing away. "Good luck with your new restaurant, Jonah," she told him. "I...hope it's everything you ever wanted."

And she hoped it was worth it. For both their sakes.

By the time she walked back to town, she knew that there was only one place she wanted to be. The bakery was closed, Jill had finished prepping for the morning, and the kitchen was dark. She let herself in through the back door and flicked on the lights, then she pulled some flour and sugar canisters onto the center island and began making one of Nana's tried and true recipes: lemon meringue pie. When life gave you something sour, she always knew how to turn it into something sweet. Becca could only hope to do the same.

She didn't even realize she'd left the back door open until she saw Jonah standing on the other side of the screen, giving her a jump.

"You scared me," she scolded him, but she was mad at him for so much more than that.

"You didn't let me explain," he said, his tone implying that he wasn't going to leave without having his say.

She set down her wooden spoon and turned to face him, folding her arms across her chest.

"I'm not leaving town," Jonah said, surprising her.

She stared at him for a moment, trying to make sense of this. Realizing that he was right. That she hadn't let him explain. That maybe, she'd gotten things all wrong.

That maybe, it wasn't for the first time.

"But...the house. Why did you list it for sale?"

"Because I am moving, just not into that house," Jonah said. "I found something better. Something closer to my family."

She tipped her head. "Closer than your grandfather's home? But he's moving in with my grandmother—right next door!"

"And don't you think they might like some space?" Jonah raised an eyebrow, and despite all the emotions and confusion roiling through her, they shared a smile.

"Besides," he said. "That was never my home. It was my home when my real home was taken from me when my parents died. All this time, I've been searching for a way to feel connected to my roots again and it was right there in front of me the entire time."

Becca stared at him through the screen, not following.

"I'm taking over my parents' old restaurant."

Now she felt her eyes widen. "But you never wanted to go in there until you had to."

He nodded in agreement. "I didn't. But it wasn't just because of what they did to the place. It was because...I thought it would hurt too much."

She felt her arms drop to her sides now, and the ache in her chest became replaced with something else. Something she'd tried to bury and fight and even deny. It wasn't just food that bonded them together, or ambition. It was the past. Their past, and the one that came before them. The one they both couldn't let go of, even when it stood in the way of the future.

"I thought I'd be honoring my parents' dream by finishing where they left off, doing what they couldn't, but the truth is that they were happy there. We were all happy. And I don't want to forget that. I don't want to live my life waiting for something I can never have when what means the most to me is right here in front of me."

He stared at her for a moment, his gaze pleading, and she felt her eyes burn with tears.

"I don't think I could have faced it without you, Becca. But once I did...I couldn't let it go. I decided to make an offer, just to see. Just to...try. I had to try."

She gave a little smile.

"It needs a lot of work," Jonah continued. "But I'm going to live in the apartment above it, so I'll be on-site, able to oversee everything."

"That's the apartment where you were born, wasn't it?" Becca asked slowly, even though she already knew that it was. She knew all those little things about him. And what they meant.

"I don't really remember it," Jonah admitted. "But just knowing that my parents lived there when they were first starting their life together makes me feel connected to it. Like it's where I'm meant to be."

"I'm happy for you, Jonah," Becca told him, meaning every word. But knowing that it wasn't her opinion that mattered right now. "And I think your parents would be too."

"I'd like to believe that," he said.

"You should. You believed in yourself. You followed your heart."

"I did," he said, looking her deep in the eye. "And it brought me back to you. You're my home, Becca."

She pulled in a shaky breath, not daring to believe that this day might turn around.

"I made a promise to my parents, but I made a promise to you too."

He reached into his pocket and pulled out his grandmother's ring. The one that he had slipped on her finger in front of everyone at Concetti's. The one that she'd looked at, every day, for nearly a year, feeling her heart bloom each time when she thought of all that was yet to come for them.

Her heart thudded against her chest as she stared at him.

"I know better than to ask right now," he said. "But I'm hoping that somehow, someday, you might accept it. That is if we can try again."

Her mind played back the last two weeks, and then the last two years, and every year before that, all the way back to when they were just kids, and he'd first come to live next door. Two broken hearts, two kids with gaping holes, that together they'd been able to make whole again.

"It's always worth a try," she said, giving him a slow smile.

His grin widened, and her eyes blurred at the sight.

"So, do you think I can come inside now?" he asked, and she laughed, just once, as the tears spilled over.

"Yes," she said, with the same amount of enthusiasm and certainty she had spoken the same word when he'd once gotten down on one knee, with his grandmother's ring.

He stepped through the door, two years older than he'd

been when he left her, a little wiser, maybe a little more scuffed and weathered, too. But when he reached out his arms and pulled her in for a kiss, she knew that he was something else, too. Settled. And certain.

And right where he belonged.

The bridal shop held a grand reopening, and despite the strict no-food policy, Denise decided to offer cupcakes and punch outside to celebrate.

Becca finished frosting the last of the small cakes. They looked like white, sparkly clouds, nearly as pretty as the gowns that Denise had hung in her storefront window.

Becca had taken to walking past the shop again, no longer averting her eyes when she passed by, but today would be the first time she'd properly visited, and this trip was long overdue.

The doors to the boutique were open when Becca walked next door, carrying a large pastry box. Denise hurried outside to greet her and set the box of cupcakes on a small table she'd covered in a lace cloth.

"Oh, these are almost too beautiful to eat!" Denise marveled. "But I'm sure they'll drive some traffic inside. With clean hands," she added sternly, gesturing to the non-nonsense sign and the stack of napkins.

"I imagine business will be better than ever," Becca said. "Sometimes people only realize how much they want something when they think it's gone."

"How true that is." Denise nodded. "And how are you and Jonah these days? I heard he's taking over his parents' old restaurant in Mapleton!"

Becca nodded. Plans were moving quickly, and most nights she and Jonah stayed up late, talking about menu ideas, looking at fabric swatches, and considering everything from new light fixtures to the music. The jazz band was thrilled for another regular weekend gig.

"I think it's right where he was meant to be," she said.

"And you girls aren't too disappointed about the bakery?" Denise looked worried.

"We're fine," Becca assured her. "More than fine, really. We've had enough change lately, and...deep down we realized that we liked things just the way they are."

"That's how I feel about the shop." Denise gestured to the window display, which had been freshly changed for today's grand reopening, even though she'd been slowly moving back into the store for weeks. "There are some things in life we shouldn't let go of."

Becca stared at the dress in the middle, and then took a step toward the window for a closer look. Memory had distorted a few of the details. She'd forgotten about the beading at the waist, which might not have been finished in what would become her last fitting with Denise, even if she didn't know it at the time.

"My dress," she said, blinking quickly, trying to make sense of what she was seeing. "You finished it."

She turned to Denise, who was doing a poor job of containing her smile.

"But my wedding was called off. And you didn't let me pay for it." Becca looked at her in wonder. That had been years ago. "Why bother finishing it?" She considered the time. The investment. "And never selling it?"

Until now, she realized. It was in the window. The most beautiful dress that Becca had ever seen. A classic strapless bodice that billowed into a ball gown skirt, in the prettiest shade of ivory taffeta.

"Oh, that dress isn't for sale," Denise said. Then, giving Becca a little smile, she said, "It's on loan."

Becca felt her throat tighten. "Loan? But—" But so many things, Becca didn't even know where to begin.

"I see many brides in my profession," Denise said. "I've never been one myself, but that doesn't mean I don't understand true love. And I knew you'd be back for that dress one day. I've just held on to it for you, for safekeeping."

Now, Becca's shoulders sank in relief that she didn't even know she needed. "Denise. But...how were you so sure even when I'd given up?"

The woman shook her head. "I didn't know. I believed. There are some people that just need a little...help."

Becca stared at Denise as a new sensation crept in. One that felt an awful lot like suspicion. "Were you ever planning to sell this store?"

"Oh, I was!" Denise assured her, nodding quickly. "And I made sure to let Robert Quincy know my plans before anyone else."

Becca laughed, but there were tears in her eyes too. "You didn't!"

"Of course I did. I couldn't think of anyone who'd want the space more than Jonah." She arched an eyebrow. "Until you girls decided to throw your hat in the ring."

The entire scheme unfolded as Becca saw how this all could have played out.

"I'm afraid we messed up everyone's plans." Becca shook her head. All of this, for something they wouldn't have wanted in the end. Not truly.

"It couldn't have had a better ending if I'd planned it myself!" Denise hooted. Then, setting a hand on Becca's arm, she confided, "And I did do a fair bit of planning."

Becca laughed again, imagining all that must have gone into this, and how it all worked out instead.

"The two of you just needed a little nudge. And it turned out that I needed one, too," Denise confided. "At first, I had to delay my decision until I knew that you and Jonah would be okay regardless of who got the space, but then, I started thinking of how much I missed doing what I loved. When I found out that Jonah was moving forward with that space in Mapleton, it all felt meant to be. I knew that you girls would be okay with the bakery just as it is. Like me, you have an attachment to that space."

"But you told me you hadn't talked to Jonah about your decision to keep your space," Becca pointed out. "Did you know he'd pulled his offer?"

"Oh, I didn't. Not from him or Erika." Denise gave a satisfied grin. "I happen to be friends with the lead musician of the band that played at your grandmother's wedding.

Hadn't heard them in ages! They told me to find them at Jonah's new restaurant! That's when I knew that everything had fallen into place. Jonah found what he was looking for. And I did too. I belong in this shop. At least for a little while longer."

"It might not have all worked out, though," Becca remarked.

"No," Denise agreed. "But the heart always finds a way to end up where it belongs."

"I should be mad," Becca said, "but I've never felt more loved. Or happy."

"Me either," Denise said, sighing with contentment. "I thought I was ready to say goodbye to this store, but as you said, sometimes you have to almost lose something to remember what you want the most."

Becca looked up into the window at her beautiful wedding dress. And she knew—better yet, she believed—that all the good things in her life would find a way back to her. Even when she least expected it.

about the author

Olivia Miles is a *USA Today* bestselling author of women's fiction and contemporary romance. She has frequently been ranked as an Amazon Top 100 author, and her books have appeared on several bestseller lists, including Amazon charts, Barnes and Noble, BookScan, and *USA Today*. Olivia lives on the North Shore of Chicago with her family and an adorable pair of dogs.

Visit www.OliviaMilesBooks.com for more.